"You Do Feel Superior, Don't You?"

He mocked her. "Have you never made a mistake, I wonder? Have you never been tempted by love or desire, greed or ambition?"

She flushed wildly and finished mopping up the coffee. "I'm hardly a beauty contest candidate. And even if I were, men frankly don't interest me at all."

He raised a curious eyebrow. "Venom? From you? Someone has hurt you badly."

"I'm not here to be mentally dissected," she said, regaining her lost composure. "I'll get you another cup of coffee."

"And I thought you didn't run from the enemy," he mused as she left him.

But she didn't answer. She couldn't.

Dear Reader:

In times like these more and more people are turning to their faith. And they want to read about people like themselves, people who hold the same beliefs dear. If this sounds familiar, you might find that SILHOUETTE INSPIRATIONS are about people like you.

SILHOUETTE INSPIRATIONS are love stories with a difference—they are novels of hope and faith about people who have made a commitment or recommitment of their lives to Christ. And SILHOUETTE INSPIRATIONS are also wonderful romances about men and women experiencing all the joy of falling in love—romances that will touch your heart.

SILHOUETTE INSPIRATIONS—more than just a love story, a love story you'll cherish!

The Editors
SILHOUETTE INSPIRATIONS

BLIND PROMISES

Katy Currie

Published by Silhouette Books New York

America's Publisher of Contemporary Romance

SILHOUETTE BOOKS, a Division of Simon & Schuster, Inc.
1230 Avenue of the Americas New York, N.Y. 10020

Distributed by Pocket Books

ISBN: 0-671-47260-7

First Silhouette Books printing March, 1984

10 9 8 7 6 5 4 3 2 1

America's Publisher of Contemporary Romance

Printed in the U.S.A.

Chapter One

Dana came to with Mrs. Pibbs standing over her, taking her pulse. For just a moment she was back in her student nurse's class six years earlier, watching Mrs. Pibbs give pointers on nursing procedure. But when she felt the stabs of pain in her head and the bruises on her slender body, she realized that she wasn't in class. She was a patient in Ashton General Hospital.

Her face felt tight when she tried to speak, and her head throbbed abominably. "Mother . . . ?" she managed weakly.

Mrs. Pibbs sighed, laying the long, fingered young hand down on the crisp white sheet. "I'm sorry, my dear," she said gently.

Tears ran down the Nordic face, misting the soft brown eyes in their frame of tousled platinum-blond hair. She'd known before she asked the question. Her last memory was of her mother's unnatural position in the metallic tangle of the front seat. But she'd hoped . . .

"Your father is here," Mrs. Pibbs said.

Dana's hurt eyes flashed. "No," she said stiffly.

The older woman looked shocked. "You don't want to see Mr. Steele?"

Dana's eyes closed. After what her mother had confessed just before the wreck, she never wanted to see him again. "I don't feel up to it," she said tightly.

"You aren't critically injured, Nurse," Mrs. Pibbs reminded her in that tutor voice. "Just some bruises and a few deep lacerations; not even a broken bone. We're observing you because of a concussion and shock more than for any great injury."

"I know. Please, Mrs. Pibbs, I'm so tired," she pleaded.

The plump woman's hard face melted a little at the look. For all her facade of stone, she was a marshmallow inside. "All right," she agreed finally. "I'll tell him you aren't up to it. Shall I ask him anything?"

Dana blinked her eyes. "The funeral arrangements. . . . Is my Aunt Helen taking care of those, or must I . . . ?"

"Your aunt and I spoke briefly this morning. Everything is being taken care of," came the quiet reply. "It's to be tomorrow. Your aunt will be by later to explain."

Dana nodded, closing her eyes wearily. It seemed like a nightmare. If only she could wake up!

"I'll tell Mr. Steele you're indisposed," Mrs. Pibbs added formally, and left Dana alone.

Dana turned her face to the wall. She couldn't bear even the sight of her father, the sound of his name. Poor little Mandy, poor little Mandy, who hadn't the weapons to survive all alone after twenty-five years of being provided for. It was inevitable that she'd break eventually. For the first few weeks after the divorce was final, Dana had been on the lookout for it to happen. But it hadn't, not even when Jack Steele announced his marriage to one of the women he worked with, a blond, motherly woman whom Dana had only seen once.

Mandy had held on, working at a florist's shop, doing well, apparently happy and with everything to live for. Until Jack had been married three months. And then, last night, Mandy had called Dana, crying hysterically, and begged for a talk.

Dana had gone, as she always went when Mandy called, and found her mother drinking heavily.

"Let's go out to supper," Mandy had begged, her pale brown eyes watery with hot tears, her wrinkled face showing its age. "I can't bear being alone anymore. Let's go out to supper and talk. I thought you might want to come back home and live with me again."

Dana had been as floored by the state her mother was in as she was by the request. She didn't want to live at home again; she wanted her independence. But there had to be some kind way to tell Mandy that, and she was searching for it when they went out to the car.

"I'll drive," Mandy had insisted. "I'm fine, dear, really I am. Just a couple of martinis, you know, nothing heavy. Get in, get in."

At that point Dana should have insisted on driving, but she'd been upset by her mother's sudden request that she move back in and she'd climbed obediently into the front seat.

"It will be lovely having you home again," Mandy cooed as she drove them toward a nearby restaurant.

"But, Mother—" Dana began.

"Your father said you wouldn't, but I knew he was lying," Mandy had continued, unabashed. Tears had suddenly sprung from her eyes, and her hands on the wheel had trembled. "He said you were glad we'd divorced, so you could spend more time with him without . . . without having to see me at the same time. He said you hated me."

Dana remembered catching her breath and staring blankly at her mother. "I didn't!" she burst out. "I never said such a thing!"

The thin old mouth began to tremble. "He made me go along with the divorce, you know. He made me. . . . "

"Dad?" she'd queried, shocked. It hardly sounded like him, but Mandy wouldn't lie to her, surely.

"There have been other women since we married, Dana," she'd continued hotly. "He only married me because you were on the way. And he tried to make me get rid of you as soon as he found out . . ."

Dana had been devastated. She opened her mouth to speak, but her mother wouldn't let her get a word in.

"I called you tonight because I'd decided that . . . that I was going to kill myself." Mandy had laughed hysterically, and her hands on the wheel had jerked; the car had accelerated. "But then I got to thinking that I needn't do that; I needn't be alone. You could come home and stay with me. You don't need to stay in that apartment alone."

"But I'm not alone. I have a roommate." Dana had tried to reason with her.

"We'll have such fun," Mandy continued wildly. She turned her head to look at Dana. "He never wanted you, but I did. You were my baby, my little girl. . . ."

"Mama, look out!" Dana had seen the truck, but Mandy hadn't. Before she could get her fogged mind to function, the truck was on top of them. Then there was only the sound of crunching metal, splintering glass. . . .

Dana felt hot tears run down her cheeks. She wept bitterly. Not only had she lost her mother, but now she understood why there had been arguments all the time, why her parents had been so hostile toward each other. It even explained why her father hadn't come near her since the divorce. He'd only married Mandy because he'd had to. He hadn't wanted Dana, not ever. No wonder he had always been away from home. No wonder he'd never tried to build any kind of relationship with his daughter. He'd hated her because she'd forced him to marry a woman he didn't love—had never loved.

Suddenly Mrs. Pibbs walked into the room, and Dana dabbed at the tears with a corner of the sheet.

"Your father's gone," she told the young nurse, wincing at the deep lacerations on the once spotless complexion. There would be scars, although Mrs. Pibbs had determined that she wasn't going to tell Dana about that just yet; Dana had had quite enough for one day.

Dana licked her dry lips. "Thank you, Mrs. Pibbs."

"Headache?"

She managed a wan smile. "A really murderous one. Could I have something, do you think?"

"As soon as Dr. Willis makes his rounds." She checked her wristwatch. "And that will be in a very few minutes."

Dana became aware of the discomfort in her face and felt the bandages on one cheek. She started. "My face . . . !"

"You should heal very well," Mrs. Pibbs said firmly. "It was inevitable, with all that broken glass. It isn't so bad, my dear. You're alive. You're very lucky that you were wearing your seat belt."

Dana's lower lip trembled. "Mrs. Pibbs, my mother . . . Was it quick?"

The older woman sighed. "It was instantaneous, the ambulance attendants told us. Now, you rest.

Don't dwell on it, just rest. The memory will fade, the cuts will fade. It only needs time." Her eyes were sad for a moment. "Dana, I lost my mother when I was fifteen. I remember very well how it hurt. I still miss her, but grief does pass. It has to."

"If only I'd insisted on driving . . . !" Dana burst out, the tears returning. "It's all my fault!"

"No, my dear, it isn't. The truck that hit your mother's car ran a stop sign. Even if you had been driving, it would have been unavoidable." She moved forward and uncharacteristically brushed the wild blond hair away from Dana's bruised face. "The driver of the truck was only scratched. Isn't it the way of things?" she added with a sad smile.

Dana bit her lip. "Yes," she murmured.

"Jenny said she'd see you later, by the way," the older nurse added. "And Miss Ena asked about you."

Dana couldn't repress a tiny smile, even through her grief. Miss Ena had undergone a gall bladder operation days before, and was the bane of the nursing staff. But strangely, she'd taken a liking to Dana and would do anything the young nurse asked.

"Tell her, please, that I'll be back on duty Friday night," Dana said gently. "If that's all right with you."

"That depends on how well you are by then," was the stern reply. "We'll wait to see about the funeral until Dr. Willis has seen you. You have to be prepared: He may very well refuse to let you go."

Dana's eyes blurred again with hot tears. "But I must!"

"You must get well," Mrs. Pibbs replied. "I'll see you later, Nurse. I'm very busy, but I wanted to check on you. Dr. Willis will be around shortly." She paused at the door, her eyes frankly concerned as she watched the blond head settle back on the pillow. Something was wrong there, very wrong. Dana's father had said as much when he was told that she refused to see him. But he wasn't going to insist, he told Mrs. Pibbs. Dana would work it out herself.

But would she? Mrs. Pibbs wondered.

Dr. Willis stopped by thirty minutes later, and Dana was shuttled off shortly afterward to X Ray. For the rest of the day, tests were run and results were correlated, and by night the tearful young nurse was given the verdict.

"No funeral," Dr. Willis said with faint apology as he made his night rounds. "I'm sorry, Dana, but a concussion isn't something you play around with. Your head took a brutal knock. I can't risk letting you up so soon."

"Then can they postpone the funeral . . . ?" Dana asked hopefully.

He shook his head. "Your aunt is in no condition to put it off," he said bluntly. And he should know: Her Aunt Helen was his patient too. "Mandy was her only living relative, except for you. She's pretty devastated. No, Dana, the sooner it's over, the better."

"But I want to go," Dana wailed bitterly.

"I know that. And I understand why," he said gently. "But you know that the body is only the shell. The substance, the spark, that was her soul is already with God. It would be like looking at an empty glass."

The words were oddly comforting and they made sense. But they didn't ease the hurt.

Dr. Willis took her pulse and examined her eyes. "Shall I call Dick and have him come by and talk to you?" he asked when he finished, naming her minister.

She nodded. "Yes, please. It would be . . . a great help right now. Aunt Helen—is she coming to see me?"

He shook his head. "Not tonight. I've had to sedate her. The shock, for both of you, has been bad. Where's Jack? I'd have thought he'd be with you."

"My father has a family to think about," she said bitterly.

He stared at her. "You're his family too."

"Tell *him,*" she said curtly, staring back. "Because he hasn't even phoned me since the divorce. Since I left home. Since I went into nurse's training! Never!"

"I see."

"No, you don't." She looked down at the white hospital sheet. "I'm very sorry, Dr. Willis; I know you're only trying to help. But this is something I have to work out by myself."

He nodded. "If I can help, I will. I've known your family for a long time."

She smiled at him. "Yes. Thank you."

"We'll keep you for two or three days, depending on how you progress," he said gently. "I wish I could give you something for the grief. But only God can do that."

Aunt Helen came by the next morning, dressed in a wildly expensive blue suit with a peekaboo hat and looking as neat as a pin. She looked a lot like Mandy, but she was taller and thinner. And much more emotional.

"Oh, darling," she wailed, throwing herself on Dana in a haze of expensive perfume and a chiffon scarf. "Oh, darling, how horrible for us both. Poor Mandy!"

Dana, just beginning to get herself back together, lost control again and wept. "I know," she whispered. "Aunt Helen, she was so unhappy, so miserable."

"I know. I told her she never should have married that man. I warned her, but she wouldn't listen!" Aunt Helen drew away with a tearful sigh. Her brown eyes were wet with tears. "I knew the minute she told me about the divorce that she wouldn't be with us much longer. She wasn't strong enough to live alone, you know."

"Yes, I know," Dana groaned. She dabbed at her eyes with a tissue. "It all happened so quickly; she was drinking. . . . "

"They told me everything. But, darling, why did you let her drive? Didn't you realize what might happen?"

Dana felt her face stiffen. "Yes, but . . ."

"Of all the stupid things to do, and you might have just taken the keys from her in the first place." The brown eyes so like her mother's were accusing. "Why in the world did you let her drive, Dana?"

Dana couldn't even manage a reply. She reached blindly for the buzzer and pushed it. A minute later, a nurse came to the door.

"Will you show my aunt the way out, please, Nurse?" Dana asked tightly, not looking at Aunt Helen, who was obviously shocked.

The nurse knew what was going on from one look at her patient's drawn face.

"I'm sorry, but Miss Steele can't be upset; she has a concussion," the nurse said firmly. "Will you come with me, please?"

As if she'd just realized what she was saying, Helen's face was suddenly white and repentant. "Darling, I'm sorry. . . ."

But Dana closed her eyes and wouldn't look or listen. The nightmare wasn't ever going to end, it seemed, and she wondered vaguely if everyone blamed her for her mother's death. She turned her face into the pillows and cried like a child.

Her minister visited that night, after the funeral was over, and Dana poured out her heart to him.

"And it's my fault; even Aunt Helen said it's my fault," she confessed.

"It's no one's fault, Dana," he said, smiling quietly. A gentle man, he made her feel at once comforted and secure. "When a life is taken, it's only because God has decided that He has more need of that life than those attached to it here on earth. People don't die for no reason, Dana, or because it's anyone's fault. God decides the moment of death, not any one of us."

"But everyone thinks it's my fault. I should have stopped her—I should have tried!"

"And if you had, there would have been something else," he said quietly. "I strongly believe that things happen as God means them to."

"I can't see anything," she confessed wearily, "except that my mother is gone, and now I have no one. Even Aunt Helen hates me."

"Your aunt was literally in tears over what she said to you this morning," he corrected. "She wanted to come back and apologize, but she was afraid you wouldn't let her into the room. She was upset; you know how Helen is."

"What am I going to do?" Dana asked him, dabbing at fresh tears.

"You're going to go on with your life," he said simply. "That life belongs to God, you know. Your profession is one of service. Isn't that the best way to spend your grief, by lessening the pain for others?"

She felt warm inside at the thought, because nursing was so much more to her than a profession. It was a way of life: healing the sick, helping the injured, comforting the bereaved. Yes, she thought, and she smiled. Yes, that was how she'd cope.

But it was easier said than done, unfortunately.

In the days and weeks that followed, forgetting was impossible.

After the first week, time seemed to fly. Dana made the rounds on her ward, pausing to see Miss Ena, who was being difficult again. The thin old lady had demanded her injection a full hour early, but Dana only smiled and fluffed up the pillows with her usual efficiency.

"Now, Miss Ena," she said with a quiet smile, "you know I'm not going to ignore Dr. Sanders's order, and you shouldn't ask me to. Suppose I have one of the volunteers come and read to you until it's time. Would that help?"

Miss Ena's sour face brightened just a little. "Well, I suppose it would," she said reluctantly. She shifted her thin body against the pillows with a sigh. "Yes," she said in a softer tone. "Thank you, it would help."

"I know hospitals are hard on people who are used to gardening and walking in the woods and pruning shrubbery," Dana confessed, laying a hand on the thin shoulder. "But in a very little while, you'll be back on your feet and doing what you please. Just keep that in mind. Believe me, it will help the time pass much more quickly."

Miss Ena smiled faintly. "I'm not used to being laid up," she confessed. "I don't mean to be disagreeable. It's only that I hate feeling helpless."

"I know," Dana said quietly. "No one likes it." She fluffed the pillows again. "How about some television now? There's a special country music awards program on," she added, knowing the elderly woman's fondness for that kind of music.

The old woman's face brightened. "That would be nice," she said after a minute.

Dana flicked on the switch and adjusted the channel, hiding a smile from Miss Ena.

Several weeks later Dana was called into Mrs. Pibbs' office, and Dana knew without asking what the reason was.

"I'd like to forget this, Nurse," she said, lifting the letter of resignation that Dana had placed on her desk early that morning as she came on duty. "Nursing has been your life. Surely you don't mean to throw away all those years of training?"

Dana's eyes were troubled. "I need time," she said quietly. "Time to get over Mother's death, time to sort out my priorities, to get myself back together again. I . . . can't bear familiar surroundings right now."

Mrs. Pibbs leaned back with a sigh. "I understand." She pursed her lips and frowned. "If it's a change of scene that you need, I may have a suggestion for you. A friend of mine is looking for a private-duty nurse for her son. He lives in some godforsaken place near the Atlantic Coast. He's blind."

"I hadn't thought about doing private duty," Dana murmured.

"You will have to support yourself," Mrs. Pibbs reminded her. "Although the salary will be good, I must warn you that it won't be all tranquility. I understand that Lorraine's son has a black temper. He was an executive, you know, very high-powered, and an athlete to boot. He's been relegated to the position of a figurehead with his electronics company."

"The blindness, is it permanent?"

"I don't know. Lorraine is rather desperate, however," she added with a tiny smile. "He's not an easy man to nurse."

Mrs. Pibbs had made it into a challenge, and right now Dana needed that.

"Perhaps," she murmured, "it would be just what I need."

Mrs. Pibbs nodded smugly. "It might be just what Gannon needs too."

Dana looked up. "Is that his name?"

"Yes. Gannon van der Vere. He's Dutch."

Immediately Dana pictured a small man with a mustache, very blond, as memory formed the one Dutchman she'd ever had any contact with—Mr. van Ryker, who'd once been a patient at the hospital. She smiled, softening already. Perhaps he could teach her Dutch while she helped him adjust to his blindness. And in helping him, perhaps she could forget her own anguish.

That night she was combing her long platinum-blond hair when Jenny came whirling in, hairpins flying as she rushed to get out of her nurse's uniform and into a dress.

"Not going out tonight?" Jenny asked from the bathroom.

"Nowhere to go," Dana replied, smiling into the mirror. "I'm having a quiet night."

"You always have quiet nights. Why don't you come out with Gerald and me?"

"No, thanks, I'd rather catch up on my sleep. I've been called out on cases twice in the past three days. How did that little girl do—the one with pneumonia that Dr. Hames admitted?"

"She's responding. I think she'll do." Jenny came back out in a green-and-white-striped dress with matching green pumps. "Say, what's the rumor about you quitting?" she asked. Jenny had never been one to listen to gossip without going to the object of it to get at the truth. It was the thing about her that Dana admired most.

"It's true," she said reluctantly, because she liked her roommate and would miss her. "I'm waiting to hear about a job Mrs. Pibbs knows of, but I have officially resigned as of next Monday."

"Oh, Dana," Jenny moaned.

"I'll write," she promised. "And so will you. It won't be forever."

"It's your mother's death, isn't it?" Jenny asked softly. "Yes, I imagine it's rough to be where you're constantly reminded of her. And with the situation between you and your family . . ."

Dana's eyes clouded. She turned away. "I'll be fine," she managed. "Have a good time tonight," she added on a bright note.

Jenny sighed as she picked up her purse. "Can I smuggle you something when I come in? A filet mignon, a silk dressing gown, a Rolls, a man . . . ?"

Dana laughed. "How about two hours' extra sleep to put in my pocket for when old Dr. Grimms calls me down to help him dress a stab wound and tells me his entire medical background before he sends me away?"

"I'll see what I can do," Jenny promised. "Good night."

"Good night."

Chapter Two

Mrs. Pibbs was waiting for Dana in her office the next morning after she'd listened to the report and was on her way to catch up on some paperwork.

"I've just talked to Lorraine," Mrs. Pibbs said with a faint smile. "She's delighted that you're going to come."

"I'm so glad," Dana replied. "Has she told Mr. van der Vere?"

"Only that a nurse is expected, I understand," the older woman replied. "It's better not to give the enemy too much information about troop movements."

Dana blinked. That old Army nurse's background popped up every so often in Mrs. Pibbs, and she tried not to giggle when it did. Surely that was a strange choice of words for a new patient. And what a very strange way to describe her impending arrival at the van der Vere home.

"Troop movements?" she asked.

"Just an expression," Mrs. Pibbs said uncomfortably. "Get on with your duties, Nurse."

Dana stared after her. A pity she didn't have time to think about that unusual description, but the doctors were due to make rounds shortly and there wasn't a minute to spare.

The week went by quickly, and before she knew it, the stitches were out of her face and she was on her way to Savannah by bus. She liked to travel cross country, preferring the sightseeing that way to airplane flights, during which she could see little more than clouds. It was early spring and the landscape was just beginning to turn green across the flat land, and she could still gaze at the architecture in each small town the bus went through. It was one of her hobbies, and she never tired of it.

The styles ranged from Greek revival to Victorian to Gothic and even Williamsburg. There were split-levels, ranch-style homes, modern, ultramodern, and apartment houses. Each design seemed to have its own personality, and Dana couldn't help but wonder about the people who lived in the houses they passed—what their lives were like.

Halfway across the state, she finally succumbed to drowsiness and fell asleep in her seat by the window. The driver was announcing Savannah when she woke up.

She took a cab out to the van der Vere summer

house. The driver followed the directions Mrs. Pibbs had given Dana, and Dana's eyes took in the jagged boulders of a new development along the beach until they drove farther and turned into a driveway lined with palms and shade trees and what looked like flowering shrubs; it was the season for them to bloom.

The house was fairly large, built of gray stone and overlooking the Atlantic, so ethereal that it might have been an illusion. Dana loved it at first sight. *It's beautiful,* she thought, *with flowers blooming all around it and the greenery profuse.*

She paid the driver and went up the cobblestone path to the door, pausing before she rang the doorbell. Well, she told herself, it was now or never. Self-consciously she tugged a lock of her loosened hair over her cheek to help conceal the scar. Bangs already hid the one on her forehead. But the worst scars were those inside, out of sight. . . .

The door opened and a small dark woman with green eyes stood smiling at her.

"You're Dana Steele?" she asked softly. "Come in, do. I'm Lorraine van der Vere; I'm so glad to meet you. Was it a long trip—were you comfortable?" she added in a rush, moving aside to let the taller woman inside.

Dana compared her own gray suit with the woman's obviously expensive emerald pantsuit and felt shabby by comparison. It was the best she had, of course, but hardly couture. If what Mrs. van der

Vere was wearing was any indication, the family was quite wealthy.

"I brought my uniform, of course," Dana said quickly. "I don't want you to think . . ."

"Don't be silly, my dear," Lorraine said kindly. "Would you like to go upstairs and freshen up before I, uh, introduce you to my son?"

Dana was about to reply when there was a crash and a thud, followed by muffled words in a deep, harsh voice. Probably a servant had dropped something in the kitchen, Dana thought, but Mrs. van der Vere looked suddenly uncomfortable.

"Here, I'll show you to your room," she said quickly, guiding Dana to the staircase with its mahogany banister and woodwork. "Come with me, dear."

As if I had any choice, Dana thought with muzzled amusement. Mrs. van der Vere acted as if she were running from wolves.

The room she was given was done in shades of beige and brown, with creamy curtains and a soft quilted coverlet in a "chocolate and spice" pattern. The carpet was thick and Dana wanted to kick off her shoes and walk through it barefoot. She took her time getting into her spotless, starched uniform. She'd wanted to put her hair up, to look more professional, but she couldn't cope with the pity in Mrs. van der Vere's eyes if those scars were allowed to show. She left off her makeup—after all, her poor patient couldn't see her anyway—adjusted her cap and went downstairs.

Mrs. van der Vere came out of the living room, hands outstretched. "My, don't you look professional," she said. "We'll have to spend some time together, my dear, once you've gotten into the routine and adjusted to Gannon." She looked briefly uncomfortable and bit her dainty lower lip. "Dana, if I may call you Dana, you . . . won't . . . that is, you're used to difficult patients, aren't you?" she asked finally.

Dana smiled. "Yes, Mrs. van der Vere . . ."

"Call me Lorraine, dear. We're going to be allies, you know."

"Lorraine," she corrected. "I was a floor nurse at Ashton General, you know. I think I can cope with Mr. van der Vere."

"Most people do, until they've met him" was the worried reply, accompanied by a wan smile. "Well"—she straightened—"shall we get it over with?"

Dana followed behind her, half puzzled. Surely the little Dutchman couldn't be that much of a horror. She wondered if he'd have an accent. His mother didn't seem to. . . .

Lorraine knocked tentatively at the door of the room next to the living room.

"Gannon?" she called hesitantly.

"Well, come in or go away! Do you need an engraved invitation?" came a deep, lightly accented voice from behind the huge mahogany door.

Lorraine opened the door and stood aside to let Dana enter the room first.

"Here's your new nurse, darling: Miss Dana Steele. Dana, this is my stepson, Gannon."

Dana barely heard her. She was trying to adjust to the fact that the small, mustached Dutchman she had been told was to be her patient was actually the man she saw in front of her.

"Well?" the huge man at the desk asked harshly, his unseeing gray eyes staring straight ahead. "Is she mute, Mother? Or just weighing the advantages of silence?"

Dana found her voice and moved forward, her footsteps alerting the tall blond man to her approach. He stood up, towering over her, his shaggy mane of hair falling roguishly over his broad forehead.

"How do you do, Mr. van der Vere?" Dana asked with more confidence than she felt.

"I'm blind—how do you think I do, Miss Steele?" he demanded harshly, his deep voice cold and cutting, his unseeing wintery eyes glaring at her. "I trip over the furniture, I turn over glasses, and I hate being led around like a child! Did my stepmother tell you that you're the fifth?" he added with a bitter laugh.

"Fifth what?" she asked, holding on to her nerve.

"Nurse, of course," he replied impatiently. "I've gone through that many in a month. How long do you expect to last?"

"As long as I need to, Mr. van der Vere," she replied calmly.

He cocked his head, as if straining to hear her. "Not afraid of me, miss?" he prodded.

She shifted her shoulders. "Actually, sir, I'm quite fond of wild animals," she said with a straight face, while Lorraine gaped at her.

A faint movement in the broad face caught her attention. "Are you presuming to call me a wild animal?" he retorted.

"Oh, no, sir," Dana assured him. "I wouldn't flatter you on such short acquaintance."

He threw back his head and laughed. "Nervy, aren't you?" he murmured. "You'll need that nerve if you stay here long." He turned away and found the corner of the desk, easing himself back into his chair.

"Well, I'll leave you two to . . . get acquainted," Lorraine said, seizing her opportunity. She backed out the door with an apologetic smile at Dana, and closed it behind her.

"Would you like to get acquainted with me, Miss Nurse?" Gannon van der Vere asked arrogantly.

"Oh, definitely, sir. I do consider it an advantage to get to know the enemy."

He chuckled. "Is that how you see me?"

"That's obviously how you want to be seen," she told him. "You don't like being nursed, do you? You'd much rather sit behind that great desk and brood about being blind."

The smile faded and his gray eyes glittered sightlessly toward the source of her voice. "I beg your pardon?"

"Have you been out of this house since the accident?" she asked. "Have you bothered to learn braille, or to walk with a cane? Have you seen about getting a seeing-eye dog?"

"I don't need crutches!" he shot back. "I'm a man, not a child. I won't be fussed over!"

"But you must see that the only recourse you've given your stepmother is to find help for you . . ." she said, attempting reason. ". . . if you won't even make the effort to help yourself."

He lifted his nose in what Dana immediately recognized as the prelude to an outburst of pure venom.

"Perhaps I would if I could be left alone long enough," he replied in a voice so cold it dripped icicles. "I've been 'helped' out of my mind. The last nurse my stepmother brought here had the audacity to suggest that I might benefit from a psychiatrist. She left in the middle of the night."

"I can see you now, flinging her out the front steps in her bedclothes," Dana retorted, unperturbed.

"Impertinent little creature, aren't you?" he growled.

"If you treat your employees this way, Mr. van der Vere, I'm amazed that you still have any," she said calmly. "Now, what would you like for dinner and I'll show you how to start feeding yourself. I assume you don't like being spoon-fed . . . ?"

He muttered something harsh and banged his fist down on the desk. "I'm not hungry!"

"In that case I'll tell the cook not to bother preparing anything for you," she said cheerfully. "When you need me, do call."

She started out the door, trying not to hear what he was saying to her back.

"Sticks and stones, Mr. van der Vere," she reminded him sweetly as she opened the door.

He growled something in another language and followed it with a slam of something on the big wooden desk. Dana smiled secretly as she closed the door behind her. Challenge, was that what had been said about this job? It would certainly be that, she affirmed silently.

Chapter Three

Lorraine was waiting for her in the hall, wringing her hands. Her small face was heavily lined with apprehension.

"Now, dear," she began nervously, "he's not at all as horrible as he seems, and I don't mind raising your salary . . . !"

Dana laughed heartily. "Oh, that won't be necessary. You couldn't pay me to leave now. It would be like retreating, and a good nurse never retreats under fire."

The older woman was visibly relieved. "Oh" was all she managed to say.

"But I can certainly understand why my predecessors were in such a rush to get out the door," she added with a grin. "He does have a magnificent temper, doesn't he?"

Lorraine sighed. "Yes, he does. Blindness isn't easy for a man like my stepson, you know. He is—was—so athletic. He especially liked water-skiing and snow skiing and aerobatics in his plane. . . ."

The other woman was painting a picture of a man who had enjoyed a reckless life-style, as if he hadn't considered life precious enough to safeguard.

She frowned. "Dangerous sports."

"Very obviously," Lorraine said quietly. "He's been that way since his wife died in the automobile wreck. He was driving, you see. It was many years ago, but he's never been the Gannon he was when I married his father."

"How old was he when you married?" she asked quietly, sensing a kindred spirit.

"He was ten." She sighed, smiling. "His mother died when he was born, and his father went to his own grave loving her. I was a substitute. He cared for me," she said quickly. "But not in the same way he cared for Gannon's mother." She turned away, as if her own memories were painful. "Is your room all right, my dear?"

"It's lovely. I'll enjoy it very much while I'm here. Mrs. van der Vere, exactly what is the problem with your stepson's eyes? Mrs. Pibbs was rather vague, and I'd like to know."

"That's the problem," Lorraine said as she led the way into her small sitting room and took a chair overlooking the rocky coastline. "There is no medical reason for his blindness. They call it—what's that word?—ideopathic. Gannon's doctor said that it could very well be hysterical blindness, brought about by the sudden shock of expecting to be stabbed in the eyes by those ragged wooden beams at the shore. The woman who was driving the speedboat lost control," she explained. "Gannon was slung toward a dock with splintered boards. How it missed his eyes was truly a miracle, but he didn't expect it to miss, you see. He was twisted and his head smashed into the dock. When he came to in the hospital, he was blind."

"And he doesn't like the idea of admitting that it could be hysterical paralysis of the optic nerve," Dana concluded, pursing her lips. "That's quite understandable, of course. Was there any emotional trauma in his life at about the same time?"

"Not that I know of," the smaller woman commented. "Of course, Gannon is a very private person."

Dana nodded. "Does he go out at all?"

"Socially, you mean? No," she said sadly. "He stays in the living room and harasses his vice-presidents over the phone."

"His vice-presidents?"

"At the electronics firm he owns, my dear. They manufacture all sorts of communications equipment—interfaces for computers, buffers, monitors, that kind of thing." She shrugged and smiled apologetically. "I don't pretend to understand; it's far too technical for me. But the company's introduced some revolutionary new system components, and apparently my stepson is something of an electronics genius. I'm very proud of him. But I have to admit, I have no idea exactly what he does."

"I don't know anything about computers," Dana murmured. She smiled secretly. "But if I asked, he might be tempted to educate me. It might even break the ice."

"Be careful that you don't fall in," Lorraine cautioned. "Gannon doesn't particularly like women right now. He was almost engaged when the accident happened. The woman walked out on him." She grimaced. "Perhaps some of that was guilt. She was driving the speedboat, you see."

Dana pondered that for the rest of the day. Poor lonely man: *His* life hadn't been any picnic so far, either. She smiled, just thinking about the challenge Gannon was going to present.

After letting him simmer all day, Dana took Gannon's dinner tray in herself.

He was sitting in a deep armchair by the open window that led onto the balcony. Outside, the waves were crashing slowly against the shore.

He lifted his shaggy blond head when he heard the door open and close. "Mother?" he called shortly.

"Hardly," Dana replied. She put the tray on the big desk, watching him stiffen at the sound of her voice.

"You again? I thought you'd gone home, Nurse."

"And leave you all alone, Mr. van der Vere?" she exclaimed. "How cowardly!"

He lifted his chin aggressively. "I don't need another nurse. I don't want another nurse. I just want to be left alone."

"Loneliness—take it from me—is bad for the soul," she said matter-of-factly. "It shrivels it up like a prune. Why don't you walk along the beach and listen to the waves and the sea gulls? Are you afraid of sea gulls, Mr. van der Vere? Do you have a feather phobia or something?"

He was trying not to laugh, but he lost. It rolled out of him like deep thunder, but he quickly stifled it. "Impertinent Miss Steele," he muttered. "Your name suits you. Are you cold and hard?"

"Pure marshmallow," she corrected, removing the lids from the dinnerware. "Just take a whiff of this delicious food. Steak and mashed potatoes and gravy, homemade rolls and buttered asparagus."

"All my favorites," he murmured. "What did you do, bribe Mrs. Wells to fix it? She hates the smell of asparagus."

"So she told me," she said with a smile. "But it was her night off. I cooked it."

"You cook?" he asked curtly.

"I used to live alone. I'd starve to death if I didn't. Now, if you can't manage by yourself, I'll be glad to spoon-feed you. . . ."

He said something unpleasant, but he got to his feet and stumbled toward the desk.

She walked around it and caught his hand. He tried to free himself but she held firm, determined not to let him dominate her.

"I'm offering to help you," she said quietly,

staring up at his scowling face. "That's all. One human being to another. I'd do the same for man, woman, or child, and I think you would for me if our situations were reversed."

He looked shocked for a minute, but he stopped struggling. He let her guide him to his chair behind the desk. But before he sat down, his big hands caught her thin shoulders for a minute and moved upward to her neck and her face and hair. He nodded then and let go of her to drop into the big chair, which barely contained him.

"I thought you'd be small," he said after a minute, groping for the cup of hot black coffee she'd placed within his reach.

"In fact, I'm above average height," she returned. The feel of his warm, strong hands had made her feel odd, and she wasn't sure she liked it.

"Compared to me, miss, you're small," he said firmly. "What color is your hair, your eyes?"

"I have blond hair," she said. "And brown eyes."

"An unusual combination." He picked up his fork and managed to turn over the coffee with one sudden movement. A torrent of words poured out of him.

"Stop that," Dana said sharply. "I'll walk right out the door if you continue to use such language around me."

"I must remember to search my mind for better words if it will get you out of my hair," he said with malicious enjoyment. "Are you such a prude, little Nurse?"

"No, sir, I am not," she assured him. "But I was always told that a repertoire of rude language disguised a pitiful lack of vocabulary. And I believe it."

He appeared to be taken aback by the comment. "I'm a man, Miss Steele, not a monk. The occasional word does slip out."

"I've never understood why men consider it a mark of masculinity to use shocking language," she replied. "I don't consider it so. Not that, nor getting drunk, nor driving recklessly. . . ."

"You should have joined a nunnery, miss," he observed. "Because you are obviously not prepared to function in the real world."

"I find the real world incredibly brutal, Mr. van der Vere," she said quietly. "People slaughtering other people, abusing little children, finding new ways to kill, making heroes of villains, using sensationalism as a substitute for good drama in motion pictures. . . . Am I boring you? I don't find cruelty in the least pleasurable. If that makes me unrealistic, then I suppose that I am one."

"It amazes me that you can stand the company of poor weak mortals, Nurse, when you are so obviously superior to the rest of us," he said, leaning back in his chair.

She felt the shock go all the way to her toes. "Superior?" she echoed.

"You do feel superior?" he mocked. "Have you never made a mistake, I wonder? Have you never been tempted by love or desire, greed or ambition?"

She flushed wildly and finished mopping up the coffee. "I'm hardly a beauty contest candidate," she said curtly. "And even if I were, men frankly don't interest me at all."

He raised a curious eyebrow. "Venom from the little nun? Someone has hurt you badly."

"I'm not here to be mentally dissected," she said, regaining her lost composure. "I'll get you another cup of coffee."

"And I thought you didn't run from the enemy," he mused as she left him.

But she didn't answer. She couldn't.

The new environment and sparring with her patient had kept Dana's mind occupied during the day, but the night brought memories. And the memories brought a gnawing ache. It was hard to believe that Mandy was gone. Sweet little Mandy, who could be maddening and endearing all at once.

She sat by the darkened window of her room and stared blankly down to where the whitecaps were visible even at night. Why did people have to die, she asked silently. Why did it all have to end so suddenly? All her life her mother had been there when she needed someone to talk to, to confide in, to be advised by.

The divorce had been no surprise when it came. The only unexpected thing was that it had taken so many years for her parents to admit that the marriage was a failure. Dana's earliest memories were of arguments that seemed to last for days, interspersed with frozen silences. Fortunately she had had grandparents who kept her each summer, and their small farm became a refuge for the young girl who felt neither wanted nor loved by her parents. Even now, with her mother dead, nothing had changed between Dana and her father. She sighed bitterly. Perhaps it would have been different if she'd been the son her father really wanted. Or perhaps it wouldn't have been.

She got up and dressed for bed. One thing was for certain, she thought as tears welled up in her eyes and spilled over: She was an orphan now. She might as well give them both up, because it was perfectly obvious that her father had no place for her in his life anymore. Her father's remarriage hadn't been such a trauma, because they hardly communicated in the first place. But to lose her mother so soon afterward, with the shock of Mandy's confession that she was going to end it all because of her husband's remarriage, was more than she could bear. There had been no time to adjust to either change in her life. No time at all.

She put out the light and crawled between the covers. *Oh, Mandy.* She wept silently. *Mandy, why did you have to go and leave me alone? Now I have no one!*

Tears soaked the pillow. She wept for the mother she didn't have anymore; for the father she'd never had. For the future, all bleak and painful and empty. But there was no one to hold her while she cried.

* * *

The next morning Gannon was sitting on the balcony when she carried in his breakfast. The wind was ruffling his blond hair, lifting it, teasing it, and she wondered suddenly how many women had done that. He had wonderful hair, thick and pale and slightly wavy.

"Breakfast," she called cheerfully, placing the tray on the table beside his chair at the edge of the balcony. The outdoor furniture was white wrought iron, and it fit the isolation and the rustic charm of the place.

Gannon half turned, and his pale gray eyes stared blankly toward her. His shirt, worn with tan slacks, had in its multicolored pattern a shade of gray that exactly matched his pale eyes.

"Must you sound so disgustingly cheerful?" he asked curtly, scowling. "It's just past dawn, I haven't had my coffee and right now I hate the whole world."

"And a cup of coffee will help you love it?" She laughed softly. "My, my, you're easy to please."

"Don't get cute, Joan of Arc," he returned harshly. He propped his long legs on another chair and sighed heavily. "Put some cream and sugar in that coffee. And how about a sweet roll?"

"How about that," she murmured, casting an amused glance at his dark face. "I brought you bacon and eggs. More civilized. More protein."

"I want a sweet roll."

"I want a house on the Riviera and a Labrador retriever named Johnston, but we don't always get what we want, do we?" she asked, and placed the plate in front of him, rattling the utensils against it loudly.

His chiseled lips pursed angrily. "Who's the boss here, honey, you or me?"

"I am, of course, and don't call me honey. Would you like me to direct you around the plate?" she asked politely.

"Go ahead. I won't promise to listen," he added darkly. He leaned forward, easing toward the coffee cup, and picked it up while she told him what was located where on his plate.

"Why can't I call you honey?" he asked when she started to go back into the house.

She stopped, staring down at him. "Well, because it isn't professional," she said finally.

He laughed mirthlessly. "No, it isn't. But if you're blond, I imagine your hair looks like honey, doesn't it? Or is it pale?"

"It's quite pale," she said involuntarily.

"Long?"

"Yes, but I keep it put up."

"Afraid some man might mistake loosened hair for loosened morals, Joan?" he mocked.

"Don't make fun of morality, if you please," she said starchily. "Some of us are old-fashioned enough to take offense."

With that she marched back into the house, while he made a sound like muffled laughter.

That afternoon he told her he wanted to walk along the beach, a pronouncement so profound that his stepmother caught her breath when she overheard it. Dana only grinned as she took his arm to lead him down the steps to the water. She was just beginning to enjoy this job.

"What changed your mind?" she asked as she guided him along the beach by his sleeve.

"I decided that I might as well take advantage of your expertise before you desert me," he said.

She glanced up at him curiously. "Why would I desert you?"

"I might not give you the choice." He stuck his free hand in his pocket and the muscles in his arm clenched. "I'm not an easy man. I don't take to blindness, and my temper isn't good at its best."

"How long have you had this problem?" she asked, doing her impression of a Viennese psychiatrist.

He chuckled at the mock accent. "My temper isn't my problem. It's the way people react to it."

"Oh, you mean those embarrassing things they do, like diving under heavy furniture and running for the hills when you walk through the door?"

"Such a sweet voice to be so sarcastic," he chided. His hand suddenly slid down and caught hers, holding it even when she instinctively jerked back. "No, no, Nurse; you're suppose to be guiding me, aren't you? Soft little hand, and strong for one so small."

"Yours is enormous," she replied. The feel of those strong, warm fingers was doing something odd to her breathing, to her balance. She wanted to pull free, but he was strong.

"A legacy from my Dutch father," he told her. "He was a big man."

"You aren't exactly a dwarf yourself," she mused.

He chuckled softly at that comment. "I stand six foot three in my socks."

"Did you ever play basketball?" she asked conversationally.

"No. I hated it. I didn't care for group sports so much, you see. I liked to ski, and I liked fast cars. Racing. I went to Europe every year for the Grand Prix. Until this year," he added coldly. "I will never go again, now."

"You have to stop thinking of your blindness as permanent," she said quietly.

"Has my mother handed you that fairy tale, too, about the blindness being hysterical?" he demanded. He stopped to face her, his hands moving up to find her upper arms. "Do I seem to you to be prone to hysterics, Nurse?"

"It has nothing to do with that, Mr. van der Vere, as I'm sure your doctor explained to you. It was simply a great shock to the optic nerve. . . ."

"I am blind," he said, each word cutting and deliberate. "That is not hysteria; it is a fact. I am blind!"

"Yes, temporarily." She stood passively in his bruising grasp, watching his scowling face intently, determined not to show fear. She sensed that he might like that, making her afraid. "It isn't unheard of for the brain to play tricks on us, you know. You saw the splinters coming straight for your eyes, and you were knocked unconscious. It's possible that your . . ."

"It is not possible," he said curtly, and his grip increased until she gasped. "The blindness occurred because I hit my head. The doctors simply have not found the problem. They invent this hysterical paralysis to spare their own egos!"

It wasn't possible to reason with a brick wall, she told herself. "Mr. van der Vere, you're hurting me," she said quietly.

All at once, his hands relaxed, although they still held her. He smoothed the soft flesh of her arms through the thin sleeves of her white uniform. "I'm sorry. I didn't mean to do that. Do you bruise easily, Miss Steele, despite your metallic name?"

"Yes, sir, I do," she admitted. He was standing quite close, and the warmth of his body and its clean scent were making her feel weak in the knees. She was looking straight up at him, and she liked the strength of his face, with its formidable nose and jutting brow and glittering gray eyes.

For just an instant his hands smoothed slowly, sensuously, up and down her arms. His breath quickened. "How old are you?" he asked suddenly.

"I'm twenty-four," she said breathlessly.

"Do you know how old I am?" he asked.

She shook her head before she realized that he couldn't see the motion. "No."

"I'm thirty-seven. Nearly thirteen years your senior."

"Don't let that worry you, sir; I've had geriatrics training," she managed to say pertly.

The hard lines in his face relaxed. He smiled,

genuinely, for the first time since she'd been around him. It changed his whole face, and she began to realize the kind of charm such a man might be able to affect.

"Have you, Saint Joan?" he murmured. He chuckled. "Have you ever been married?"

"No, sir," she said, aware of the primness of her own soft voice.

His head tilted up and an eyebrow arched. "No opportunities?" he murmured.

She flushed. "As you accused me, Mr. van der Vere, I'm rather prudish in my outlook. I don't feel superior, I just don't believe in shallow relationships. That isn't a popular viewpoint these days."

"In other words you said no and the word got around, is that what you mean, miss?" he asked quietly.

It was so near the truth that she gaped up at him. "Well, yes," she blurted out.

He only nodded. "Virtue is a lonely companion, is it not?" he murmured. He let go of her arms, and before she realized what he was doing, he framed her face with his big, warm hands. "I want to know the shape of your face. Don't panic," he said.

But she didn't want him to feel that long, ugly scar down her cheek, and she drew away as if he'd struck her sharply.

His face hardened. "Is it so intimate, the touch of hands on a face?" he asked curtly. "Pardon me, then, if I offend you."

"I'm not offended," she said stiffly, standing apart from him on legs that threatened to buckle.

His touch had affected her in an odd way. "I just don't like being touched, Mr. van der Vere."

His heavy brows arched up. "Indeed? May I suggest, miss, that you have more inhibitions than would be considered normal for a woman of your years?"

She stiffened even more. "May I suggest that I'd rather have my inhibitions than your ill temper?"

He made a rough sound and turned away. "At any rate you flatter yourself if you think there was more than curiosity in that appraisal. I can hardly lose my head over a figure I can't even see."

The flat statement cruelly reminded them of his blindness. She felt angry with herself for denying him the shape of her face, but she hadn't wanted him to feel the scar. It had made her less than perfect and much more sensitive than usual to her lack of looks.

He started along the beach, faltering. "Are you coming, Nurse, or would you like to see me fall flat on my face in the surf?" he asked sharply.

"Don't try to make me feel guilty, Mr. van der Vere," she said, taking his arm. "I won't apologize for being myself."

"Did I ask you to?" He sighed heavily. "I hate being blind."

"Yes, I know."

"Do you?" His voice was harsh with sarcasm. "But then, you think I'm having hysterics, don't you, Nurse, so why the sympathy in your voice?"

"You won't try to understand what the term means, will you?" she shot back. "Would you rather enjoy your temporary affliction, Mr. van der Vere? Does it please you to hurt other people out of your own refusal to help yourself?"

He seemed to grow taller, and his face became rigid, like stone. "If you were a man . . ." he began hotly.

"If I were a man, I'd be an archaeologist," she said pleasantly, "out digging up old bones. I wouldn't be a nurse, so I wouldn't be here, and you'd have no one to yell at then, would you?"

He said a rough word under his breath and his chiseled lips made a thin line. At his sides his powerful hands clenched convulsively.

"Would you like to go swimming with me, Miss Steele?" he said after a minute.

"No, sir, I would not. And shame on you for what you're thinking. The shark would only get indigestion."

He seemed to be muffling a laugh, but he couldn't stop the sound that burst from his throat. It was a delightful sound, full of rich humor and love of life. It was like music to Dana's ears.

"Lead me home, if you please," he chuckled. "The sea is too tempting, I confess."

"It's for your own good that I prod you, sir," she said as they walked along the beach. "Self-pity is self-defeating, you know."

"Was I feeling sorry for myself?" he mused. He stumbled, cursed and pulled himself erect. "Stop leading me into rocks."

"That was a piece of driftwood, and if you'd pick up your feet instead of shuffling along, disturbing sand crabs, you wouldn't trip," she returned with a grin.

"Witch," he accused.

"No wonder you wanted to get me in the water," she mumbled. "You wanted to find out if I'd float, right?"

He shook his head. "I think I have met my match," he murmured. "Tell me something, miss. If you and the doctors are wrong, and the blindness is not hysterical, what then? Do you move in to lead me around for the rest of my life?"

She was convinced that the doctors wouldn't have made such a mistake, not with the battery of tests that had been done. But she was weary of arguing the point.

"If they're wrong," she said, stressing the first word, "then you learn to live with it. There are fantastic developments in computer science that deal with blindness—as I'm sure you know from your involvement in that field."

"Yes, I know," he said quietly. "In fact, one of my engineers developed a braille system that allows the blind access to other blind people through their computers."

"You see? It isn't a closed door you're facing. And will you consider one other thing?"

"What?"

"That God gives us obstacles for reasons?"

"God," he said, "did not make me blind. I did that all by myself, so why should I expect Him to help me?"

"Why shouldn't you?" she countered. "I suspect you're not a religious man."

"You suspect correctly."

"What are you doing about it?" she asked. "What do you do to justify your existence?"

"I work for myself," he said gruffly.

"And for financial gain."

"Of course. What other reason is there?" he grumbled. "I am not a philanthropist."

"Obviously."

He shifted restlessly. "Don't try to toss a mantle of guilt over me. I give to charity."

"What do you give of yourself?"

He stopped dead. "I beg your pardon?"

"What do you give of yourself? Money is vulgar."

"So speaks one without it," he returned coldly. "It never ceases to amaze me that the people who complain the most about the way wealth is distributed are usually the very people who lack it."

"Touché," she agreed pleasantly, looking up at his windblown hair, his hard face. "I've been poor most of my life, Mr. van der Vere. I'd like to have an expensive dress once in a while, and I have a deep love for luxurious perfume. But I've lived very well without those things. The difference is that I live a life of service for God. My pleasure comes from the giving of myself."

He looked uncomfortable. "Then why did you give it up to come here?" he asked suspiciously. "I'm sure you're getting paid much more here than you make working in your hospital," he added sarcastically.

She glanced away from him, flushing. "That's true. But the money wasn't the reason I came."

"Then, what was?"

She straightened. "Personal reasons, Mr. van der Vere, that have nothing to do with you. Shall we go?"

"Refusing the challenge?" he prodded. "Very well, lead me back into the house. I wouldn't want the wind to dislodge your halo."

She wanted nothing more at that moment than to shake him. But that wouldn't accomplish anything. At least she'd nudged him out of his self-pity, a minor victory. Perhaps there would be others.

She walked alongside him, feeling oddly elated. She wanted to take the pins out of her long hair and let it blow free. She wanted to take off her sensible white nurse's shoes and run barefoot along the damp beach, like a child enjoying nature's beauty. Her eyes lifted to the somber man at her side. She was beginning to see a purpose in her presence there; it went much deeper than the nursing of a blind man.

Chapter Four

The next weeks were trying. Gannon van der Vere seemed to go out of his way to find fault with Dana. Nothing she did pleased him, and all the ground she seemed to have gained in the first few days abruptly slid back into the sea.

He sat behind his desk and stayed on the phone almost constantly. He refused to go out of the room except to sleep. He was irritable and unapproachable, and when Dana tried to talk to him, he found an excuse not to listen. The doctor's visit only irritated him further, and after his examination he retreated into his bedroom and wouldn't even come out to eat.

"Dr. Shane just restated his own opinion to Gannon." Lorraine sighed wearily as she and Dana sat down to supper by themselves. "It made him furious, of course. He won't accept that the condition isn't due to something surgically correctible."

"He's a stubborn man," Dana commented.

"Worse than stubborn. Just like his late father." She smiled. "He was quite a man, my husband. A little mellower than Gannon, but of course he was older."

"Perhaps he'll come to admit it eventually," Dana suggested. "In the meanwhile, having people around would help him tremendously. Doesn't he have friends?"

"He had plenty of them, when he could see," his stepmother said angrily. "And girl friends by the score. People who loved for him to spend money on them. Now . . ." She shrugged her delicate shoulders. "This place is like the end of the earth for that kind of person, Dana. They don't like peace and solitude. They like bright lights and activity and, frankly, drugs and alcohol."

"Did he?" she asked, because she wanted to know.

"Gannon?" she laughed. "No, he was never the type to need crutches of any kind. His late wife was the party-goer. Of course, I don't think she indulged. But all their friends do."

"No children?"

"They didn't want children," Lorraine said with a sigh. "Their lives were so full, you see."

Full. Dana doubted that, somehow, but she was too polite to state her convictions. She was getting a vivid picture of Gannon's life before the blindness, and it was an unpleasant one. She felt sorrier for him than ever.

Dana especially loved the beach at night, and when she could sneak away for a few minutes, she liked to walk along the shore and watch the whitecaps roll against the damp sand. Lorraine never minded her brief absences, but when Gannon discovered what she was doing, he made a point of seeking her out one Friday evening on the beach.

"Nurse!" he bellowed, pausing on the last step that led down from the house, his hand clenched on the railing.

She rushed back toward him, her loosened hair flying, afraid he'd tumble down in his anger.

"I'm here," she said breathlessly. "There's no need to yell."

"May I ask what you're doing down here?" he grumbled, staring in her general direction.

She studied his ferocious scowl while his hair and her soft green dress blew wildly in the cool ocean breeze. "I'm walking on the beach, Mr. van der Vere," she said calmly.

"On my time," he agreed.

"Excuse me, sir, I thought I had ten minutes a day to myself," she said with polite sarcasm.

"A live-in nurse is supposed to be within call every minute," he snapped.

"I was," she pointed out. "Didn't I come running?"

He drew in a sharp breath. "The beach is dangerous at night," he said after a minute, as if it annoyed him that he'd had to show any concern for her. "There are transients down the beach who like to party. You're not sophisticated enough to cope with drunken men, Miss Steele. Will you come in the house, please."

The concern touched her. Only her mother and Jenny had ever shown any for her over the years.

"Lost your tongue?" he growled after a minute.

She shrugged. "I'm not used to people worrying about me," she said finally.

He seemed to hesitate, his hand curling slowly around the banister. "Your parents do, surely?"

The question cut in a new way. She averted her gaze to the sea and tried not to cry; tears were so close to the surface these days, the grief was so raw and unfamiliar. "My mother died in a wreck a few months ago," she said softly.

"I'm sorry," he said quietly. "Your father?"

"We have very little contact," she admitted. "It's my fault as much as his. I'm not good at relationships, you see. I'm wary of letting people get close."

"Even family?" he burst out. "My God, are you fearful of contamination?"

He made her sound odd, and she didn't like it. "Fearful of being hurt, if you must know," she shot back, her eyes blazing. "I'd rather be alone than cut to ribbons emotionally, and what business is my personal life to you?"

His heavy blond brows shot straight up. "Claws," he murmured, and a corner of his mouth curved. "Well, well, you land on your feet, don't you, for all your repressed virtue."

She stared at the sand. "You irritate me," she bit off.

"We're even, because you irritate me as well. Now, will you come in, before I yield to temptation and toss you into the surf to cool you off?"

She drew in an angry breath and started past him, but his hand shot out at the sound of her steps on the stone and she was dragged against his powerful body.

Her tiny gasp was audible even above the thunderous surf, and she was aware of every cell that came in contact with him. He smelled of expensive cologne and soap, and the hand around her waist was big and very warm. His breath was on her forehead, his chest was rising and falling with a curious heaviness and her knees threatened to collapse.

He felt her hair blow against his face as it bent, and he brushed at long, silky strands of it with his free hand. "Such soft hair," he remarked quietly. "Blond?"

She swallowed. "Yes, sir." Why was her voice quavering like that? What was happening to her?

His hand brushed her shoulder and moved down her back to her shoulder blades. He drew her close with aching tenderness until her cheek was pressed against his warm, broad chest over his silky blue shirt.

She could feel the strength of him under her

hands, the hard beat of his heart. It had been a long time since any man had held her, but never had it made her feel like this. She was vulnerable all at once, womanly, feminine in a totally new way.

"You smell of wildflowers," he said, his voice deep and quiet in the semidarkness. "And your thinness frightens me. You aren't hardy; you're very fragile."

She tried to breathe normally. "I'm not fragile," she protested weakly. Her hands pressed palm down over the warm muscles of his chest, half in protest. "Mr. van der Vere . . ."

"Isn't it ethical, little moralist?" he mused. "I thought comfort was your stock-in-trade."

"Comfort?"

His cheek nuzzled against hers. "I've been alone a long time," he said in a low whisper. "Without touching, or being touched. Sometimes just the scent of a woman is enough to drive me half mad. . . ."

She jerked away from him all at once, frightened of the sensuality she could hear in his voice, feel in his warm hands on her back. She put herself a safe distance away and tried to stop shaking.

"It's getting cold out here," she murmured.

"Ice cold," he said harshly. "Little Nun, why don't you join a convent?"

"I'm not on offer as a woman, Mr. van der Vere!" she burst out, furious at his casual approach. "I'm a nurse; it's my job, it's why I'm here! If you're thinking of adding anything personal to my duties, you'd better start running ads fast: I quit!"

"Wait!"

She froze a step above him, listening as he felt for the banister and started up the steps behind her, stopping when he felt her body was just ahead of him.

"All right, I'm sorry," he said shortly. "I only meant to tease, not to run you off. I'm . . . getting used to you. Don't leave me."

The stiff pride got through to her when nothing else would have. She turned around and looked at his set features with softening eyes. It must indeed be hard for such a man, used to such a life-style, to endure the loneliness of this isolated beach house. Could she blame him for reacting to the first young woman he'd been near in months?

She drew in a slow breath. "I won't leave you," she said quietly. "But you've got to stop making dead sets at me if I stay. I won't be treated like a temporary amusement, especially by a patient. I take my nursing seriously: It isn't a game to me; neither is it an opportunity for a little holiday romancing on the side."

"You speak bluntly," he replied. "May I?"

"Yes, sir."

"I have been without a woman for many months, and I'm not suited to the life of a hermit." His shoulders lifted and fell. "I had no intention—have no intention," he rephrased, "of treating you like an amusement. I simply wanted a woman in my arms, for a moment. I wanted to feel like a man again." He shifted restlessly. "Lead me up, will you? I'm tired."

He seemed to slump, and tears burned her eyes. She hadn't thought of how barren his emotional life would be because of the blindness, and she felt cold at her harsh rejection of him. She'd misunderstood; now she felt guilty.

"I'm sorry I snapped," she said, taking him by the arm. "I . . . I didn't understand. I'm a little afraid of men, I think. My fear makes me overreact."

"Afraid?" he asked curiously.

"I've led a sheltered life," she confessed. "I don't even know how to protect myself. Men are very strong. . . ."

"You make me sound like a potential mugger," he ground out. "I wouldn't attack you!"

"How reassuring; I was worried to death about that," she said with a teasing laugh.

All his bad humor disappeared at once. "I'll bet you were," he muttered. He found her hand and clasped it in his, and she felt a strange little shock of pleasure at the warm strength of it. "Nothing personal, Nurse; I only need to be led and I can hold on to you more easily like this. All right?"

She looked down at his brown hand holding hers. "All right," she said meekly. It wasn't professional, of course. But it was . . . practical.

He was easier after that, more approachable, regaling her with stories of his travels while she took him walking and driving in the car and tried to ease him out of his cold shell. Some of the tales he recounted were frankly shocking, and she began to wonder at the wildness of the life he'd lead.

"What about your own life?" he asked while they were drinking coffee at a local restaurant. Their table overlooked the ocean, and Dana picked at her apple pie while her eyes drank in the blueness of the water, the whiteness of the beach, dotted with swimmers in their colorful bathing suits.

"Hmmmm?" she murmured dreamily.

He made an impatient sound. "Are you worshipping the view again? Lorraine said you watch the ocean as if you're afraid it may vanish any second."

"I love it," she said sheepishly. "We don't have oceans around Ashton, you know. Just open land and a lot of farms and cattle."

"How big is Ashton?"

"About five thousand people," she told him. "It isn't far south of Atlanta, but it's mostly rural. I grew up there. I know most everybody else who did too."

"Is that one of those towns where the sidewalk draws in at six and everything closes for the night?"

"Very nearly. We don't even have a bowling alley. Although," she added, "we do have a theater and a skating rink."

"How exciting," he mused. "No bars?"

"We're in a dry county," she replied.

"You don't drink, I gather."

She sighed, watching the ocean again. "Mr. van der Vere, I never have. I'm sure my life is duller than dishwater compared to yours."

He lifted his coffee to his chiseled mouth, frowning slightly. "My world was an endless round of parties, cruises, business conventions, casinos and first-class travel. It was never dull."

She tried to imagine a life-style so hectic, and failed. "Were you happy?"

He blinked, staring in her direction. "Happy?"

"I can look it up in the dictionary and read you the definitions, if you like," she murmured.

"I was busy," he corrected, idly caressing the coffee cup. "Occupied. Entertained. But happy?" He laughed shortly. "What is happiness, Nurse? Tell me."

"Being at peace inside yourself, liking yourself and the whole world all at once," she said simply. "Going about your work with your whole heart and loving what you do."

"You're talking about a feeling," he said, "not the trappings that go with it."

"Exactly. I could be just as happy working in a sewing plant or digging in a garden as I am nursing, if it fulfilled me," she told him.

"I imagine a family could provide you with the same sense of purpose," he remarked. "Have you not wanted a husband and children?"

She toyed with her pie and laid down the fork to pick up her coffee. "Mr. van der Vere," she said after a minute, "I'm a very plain woman. I have rigid views on life and the living of it. I don't have casual affairs, I work hard and I keep to myself. It's very unlikely that I'm ever going to find a man dumb enough to marry me."

He sat up straight. "You spend so much time running yourself down, Miss Steele," he said after a minute, scowling toward her. "Is it deliberate, calculated to keep people at arm's length?"

She laughed. "I suppose so. I like my life, why change it?"

"Yet, you seem determined to change mine," he reminded her.

"That's different. Yours needs changing," she said pertly. "You were about to go into permanent hibernation, and frankly, Mr. van der Vere, you're not the best companion in the world to hibernate with. You'd have driven yourself crazy."

He burst out laughing, his voice deep and amused, the sound of it like silver bells in the darkness. "And you're sacrificing yourself to tend me, no doubt."

"Of course," she returned, joining in the game. "Think of all the other people in the world I could inflict myself on!"

He seemed about to say something, then thought better of it. He finished his coffee in one swallow. "I wish I could see you," he said surprisingly. "I wonder if you really are as plain as you like to pretend."

She thought about the scar on her cheek and lifted her eyes to his broad, hard face. "Yes," she said softly. "I am."

His mouth broke into a smile. "Beauty is only skin deep, they say, miss."

"Yes, sir," she sighed, "but ugly goes all the way to the bone, doesn't it?"

He laughed loudly, and the sound was infectious. She laughed with him, wondering at the easy comradeship of their developing relationship. He was like another man, and she felt herself changing. Despite her neat nurse's uniform, which seemed to be drawing its share of curious stares, the woman inside it was being drawn inexplicably closer to the big blond man across from her.

They passed a wreck on the way back to the beach house. Dana paled as she watched ambulance attendants drag an unconscious form from the tangle of metal and glass, but she didn't make a big thing of it. The rest of the way back she talked about the scenery and described houses and beach property to him. But inside she was reliving every minute of the wreck that had killed her mother.

That night it was inevitable that the nightmare would come. She saw the truck coming toward her, felt the impact, saw the unearthly position of her mother's body. . . .

Someone was shaking her roughly; a deep voice was cursing as her eyes flew open. She shook her head, breathing raggedly, and found Gannon and Lorraine standing by the bed. Gannon was wearing a dark robe over his pajamas, and Lorraine was clutching a delicate pink negligee around her, her face troubled.

"We heard you scream, dear. Are you all right?" Lorraine asked, concerned.

Dana sat up, trying to calm her wild heartbeat. Her eyes were full of tears, and she felt sick all over. "It was just . . . just a nightmare. I'm sorry I disturbed you both."

"It's all right," Lorraine said. "We were worried. Will you be. . . ?"

"I'll sit with her for a moment," Gannon said curtly, ramming his hands into his pockets. "Would you have the maid fix some coffee and bring it up?"

"I'll do it myself," Lorraine said, turning. "I could use a cup, too. Back in a minute."

"You don't have to stay with me. . . ." Dana said tautly.

He felt his way to the chair by the bed and sank into it. His blond hair was tousled, his face was grim, his blind eyes bloodshot, as if he hadn't slept at all. His pajama top and robe had fallen open over a mat of blond hair that seemed to cover his broad chest, and he looked impossibly masculine in her bedroom. He made her nervous.

Oddly enough, he seemed to be concerned about her. He looked toward her, his eyes troubled. "I won't leave you, Dana," he said quietly, and the sound of her given name on his lips disturbed and flattered her.

She pushed back her long hair with a ragged sigh and dabbed at the tears with a corner of the sheet. "I should get up," she murmured, tossing back the covers to reach for her robe at the foot of the bed. It was blue terrycloth, and old, but it made her feel more secure with a man in the room—even a sightless one.

"Self-conscious?" he asked gently. "You aren't

used to men seeing you in your nightclothes, are you? Not that I can see. . . ." he growled. "Are you all right? What happened?"

"I had a nightmare, that's all," she said, and the mattress sprung up as she got to her feet and tied the robe securely.

He stood up at the same time, colliding with her. She gasped and clung to him to keep her balance, and the magic of his warmth and strength made her knees even weaker.

"Dana?" he whispered, bending.

Incredibly, he found her knees and back and lifted her completely off the floor in his arms, holding her to his chest.

"Mr. . . . van der Vere . . ." she protested.

"My name is Gannon," he breathed, searching blindly for her mouth. "Say it. . . ."

"Gannon . . ."

His lips took his name from hers, and she felt their warm, soft pressure against her own with a leap of her heart. She stiffened, but when the pressure continued with the same tenderness, she let her taut muscles relax.

"That's it," he whispered. "I'm not going to hurt you. I only want to comfort you a little, that's all. Please, don't deny me the one altruistic gesture of my life."

She watched his face as he kissed her again, softly, with the same undemanding pressure as before. His mouth was warm and hard, and she liked the feel of it rubbing against her own. She liked the minty sigh of his breath on her lips and the smell of him and the strength of his arms holding her.

She let her arms slide around his neck and her mouth tentatively moved against his, a tiny movement like a tremor. He stiffened; his arms tightened. Then his brows began to knit and his face hardened. All at once his mouth burrowed between her lips and the kiss became complete.

She gasped and pushed at his shoulders, and he drew back immediately, breathing hard.

"Predictable, wasn't it, little one?" he whispered with a wry smile. "I'm sorry, I didn't mean to take liberties. I really did mean to comfort you and nothing more."

"It's all right, I understand," she said shakily. She watched his face with awe. She hadn't dreamed that a kiss could be so . . . frighteningly affecting.

"Perhaps we'd better have our coffee in more sedate surroundings after all," he murmured dryly as he set her back on her feet. "You're a temptation, miss, and you have a very sweet young mouth that I could learn to like all too well. I don't want to see you rush wildly away because I lost my head in the darkness."

She dragged her robe closer. "As you said," she replied, "it was the darkness. And my fear."

He touched her sleeve. "The wreck we saw this afternoon—it brought back unpleasant memories?"

"Yes, sir." She pushed back her hair. "Hadn't we better go? Your stepmother will have a pot of coffee by now, I expect."

"Yes, I expect so." He let her take his arm and lead him out of the room. "And I thought I was the patient," he teased softly. "Perhaps we were both mistaken."

She made a tiny sound and smiled as they joined Lorraine in the dining room.

Chapter Five

A minor crisis in Gannon's company kept him occupied on the phone for hours the next day, and an unexpected visitor arrived just as the cook was putting dinner on the table.

"Dirk!" Lorraine cried, smiling. She jumped up from the table and darted toward a tall, dark man while Dana tried to figure out who the newcomer was.

He was as dark as Gannon was fair, and not nearly as big. He had an easy smile and his face was that of a man who laughed a lot. The only Dirk whom Dana had heard mentioned during her stay at the beach house was Gannon's brother, but of course this couldn't possibly be him . . . could it?

"And who is this?" Dirk asked, when Lorraine stopped hugging him, nodding past her to where

Dana sat neatly in her nurse's uniform at the long table.

"Gannon's nurse, Dana Steele. Dana," Lorraine said with a gay smile. "This is my other stepson, Dirk van der Vere."

"I'm very pleased to meet you," Dana said politely.

He grinned, and she realized suddenly that he wasn't much older than she was. And where Gannon's Dutch accent was detectable, Dirk spoke English without the trace of an accent.

"The pleasure is all mine," he corrected. "Am I in time for dinner? Great, I'm starved."

"What brings you down here?" Lorraine asked.

"Gannon. He's in the study, as usual, I take it?" he continued, ramming his hands into the pockets of his gray suit. He sighed. "We've got a strike on our hands, and it's all my fault."

"Is it, or is Gannon just blaming you?" Lorraine murmured with a tiny smile.

He chuckled. "Know him pretty well, don't you? No, I suppose if he'd been in my shoes, he'd have averted it. That's true enough." He shrugged. "I wasn't in a position to promise too much until I could talk to Gannon."

"Can you iron it out?"

"That's what he had me fly down here to find out. Two of the union people wanted to come with me, but Gannon wouldn't allow it: He didn't want them to see him . . . like this."

"If only he weren't so sensitive about it," his stepmother sighed.

"Amen." He turned to Dana. "Making any progress?"

She laughed. "Not too much, but at least I've coaxed him out of the house a few times."

"It's just that we can't mention his blindness," Lorraine added. "He won't even listen when the doctor discusses the reason for it."

"Maybe he wants to be blind. Have you ever thought of that?" Dirk asked soberly. "No, hear me out," he continued, when the older woman would have interrupted. "You know how hard he was pushing himself before the accident. And there was Layn hanging on to him like a leech, dragging him around the world with her. . . . He was going twenty-three out of every twenty-four hours, and it was telling on him. Maybe his body did it to him to save itself."

"Layn," Lorraine said bitterly. "Where is she now, do you know?"

"Hanging around with a rich sheikh, I hear," Dirk said coldly. "Where I hope she stays. You do realize that if Gannon regained his sight, she'd be back here like a shot?"

"Surely he wouldn't take her back," the elderly woman said.

Dirk laughed. "Are you kidding? You've seen Layn; what sighted man could resist her?"

Lorraine sighed wearily. "I suppose you're right."

Dana was sitting quietly, listening. Layn must have been the woman who had walked out on him when he was blinded. According to what they were saying, he must have cared for her very much. She stared into her plate. Against a woman like that, what chance would a plain woman have with a man like Gannon van der Vere? She blinked. Why should she have such an odd thought? She didn't care about him, so what did it matter about the woman from his past?

She became aware suddenly that Dirk was watching her, but when she looked up, he grinned.

"Deep in thought, Miss Steele?" he asked. "How in the world did Gannon manage to find such an attractive nurse? This is a pretty dull place."

She flushed at the unexpected compliment. She'd thought the scar down her cheek would detract from what slight beauty she possessed, but Dirk hadn't seemed to notice it. "You're very kind," she murmured, "but I love it here."

"Dana isn't like Layn, my dear," Lorraine said with a gentle smile. "She's managed to get your brother out of the house, out of his shell. He's even allowing me to have a small party next month for his birthday—just intimate friends, you understand, but isn't it a big step in the right direction?"

Dirk chuckled. "Yes, indeed. Miss Steele must be a miracle worker of sorts," he added, winking at her. "Well, let me go and face the dragon. Then perhaps we can sit down to a peaceful meal."

He wandered off toward the study. The door opened and closed, and there was a loud discussion behind it.

Lorraine laughed softly as Dana's head lifted curiously.

"Nothing to worry about, Dana," she said. "They argue constantly, especially when it comes to company policies. Gannon would like to expand the business; Dirk is cautious. Gannon believes in the generous approach to labor negotiations; Dirk is conservative. They're very different."

"I suppose most brothers are," came the quiet reply. "I've always hated being an only child. I used to hope for a brother or sister when I was little."

"Your parents couldn't have other children?"

Dana shifted uncomfortably. "No," she said simply, letting it go at that.

"I'd better have the maid get a room ready for Dirk. No doubt he'll be here at least overnight. I never expect quick solutions when my stepsons start discussing company politics." She patted Dana on the shoulder and left the room.

It was another hour before the men joined them at the table, and Dana was starving. The beef and scalloped potatoes had been kept warm, and now fresh rolls and asparagus with hollandaise sauce was being brought in by the cook.

"That smells like asparagus," Gannon remarked as he slid cautiously into his chair at the head of the table. He looked out of humor, but Dana noted that he wasn't scowling as fiercely as usual.

"It is," Lorraine said. "Everything settled?"

Dirk only laughed. "If you believe that, I've got

some oceanfront property in Arizona I'd like to talk to you about."

"In the middle of the Painted Desert, no doubt," Dana murmured, tongue in cheek.

Dirk's eyebrows lifted. "However did you guess?"

Gannon was listening to their conversation, and his face darkened. "How long are you staying, Dirk?" he asked curtly.

"Oh, a couple of days, I suppose—now that you've phoned Dobbs and gotten the union off my back," the younger man added wryly.

Gannon made a gruff sound and waited for Dana to fill his plate and tell him what was where. The others watched the small ritual with careful amusement. It was so new for them to have Gannon docile.

Her eyes ran over his hard face like silk, liking its rough contours, the broad forehead and jutting brow over his gray eyes. He was a handsome man. Dana could almost picture him in evening clothes; he'd stand out anywhere.

Dirk, watching, smiled at the look on her face. "Dana, how would you like to drive up to Savannah with me tomorrow and see the city?"

She jerked her eyes up, astonished at the unexpected invitation. She wasn't the only one, because Gannon's eyes darkened menacingly.

"I can't spare her," Gannon said shortly.

"She's been here for several weeks, dear," Lorraine reminded him, "without a single day off. Don't you think she deserves a little recreation?"

Gannon's jaw tautened. "She's been out driving with me, hasn't she? Walking?"

"Really, Mrs. Steele, it's all right . . ." Dana began softly.

"No, it isn't," Dirk broke in. "She isn't slave labor."

Gannon made a rough sound. "All right, take her with you," he said harshly. "If she thinks she needs a day away from me, I can't stop her."

He was making her feel guilty, and she didn't like it.

"She does need a day away from here," Lorraine seconded. "She's young, Gannon; it must be terrible to be shut away from the world like this."

"But it isn't . . . !" Dana tried to say, but Gannon's deep voice drowned her words.

"Go, then," he said bitterly. "I don't need you, Miss Steele, and that's a fact. I never have." He tossed his napkin aside and almost knocked over his chair, getting to his feet. "Excuse me, I've lost my appetite."

Dana was painfully aware of the two pairs of eyes watching her, but she was too disheartened to put her thoughts into words. She felt as if she'd betrayed the big Dutchman, and it wasn't a feeling she liked. Perhaps she was getting too close to him and a day away would do her good. After all, this job was temporary. He might regain his sight any day and she'd return to Ashton.

That thought disturbed her very much. She went walking on the beach at dusk, dragging her feet in the sand, her eyes troubled as they sought the horizon across the ocean. Her disorderly mind kept going back to that warm, slow kiss they'd shared the night before, and the strange new feelings it had kindled in her. She couldn't remember ever wanting a kiss to begin again, not with any other man. But, of course, Gannon was an experienced man. She hugged her arms across her chest. She had to stop thinking about it nevertheless. She was his nurse, nothing more; she couldn't afford the luxury of getting emotionally involved with him. He was just passing time, but Dana was far too moral a woman to yield to temptation. Besides that, she didn't want him getting too close. It was a trap that would rob her of her peace of mind, that would make her vulnerable. She didn't trust emotions anymore. Especially she didn't trust her own. Her life, since her mother's death, had dissolved. She felt totally alone, and a part of her liked that aloneness. It would protect her from any more wounds; it would protect her from being hurt again.

"Dana! Wait up!"

She whirled, the wind catching her loosened hair, to find Dirk running along the beach toward her. He was wearing jeans and a knit shirt, and he was barefoot.

"You're fast, lady," he chuckled, sticking his hands in his pockets as he fell into step beside her. "What are you doing out here all alone?"

"Enjoying the view," she admitted. He was easy to talk to, and she smiled. "Isn't it just great? Sea breeze, all that ocean out there, and peace and quiet along with it. People tire me sometimes. I like solitude."

"Don't mind your own company?" he teased lightly. "You're a rarity. Most people can't stand to be alone."

"Your brother seems to like it well enough," she mused, glancing up at him. "Is it only since the blindness?"

"Exactly. Oh, he's been a lone wolf most of his life in that he lives as he pleases." He frowned. "But he's never cared for solitude like this. There were always . . . friends with him," he added, and she wondered if he meant to say *women* instead of *friends*.

"We're all different," Dana sighed. "It's a good thing too. Imagine how dull it would be if we all thought alike?"

"There'd be fewer wars," he reminded her.

"Yes, but creativity would go down the drain."

"As you say." He pursed his lips and looked down at her. "Is he making much progress?" he asked.

She let her shoulders rise and fall. The comfortable jeans and sweat shirt she was wearing felt wonderful in the cool air. "I thought so until tonight. I really don't think it's a good idea that I go to Savannah with you—not if it's going to upset him like that. It's been a struggle just getting him out of the house."

He nodded. "I can imagine. But you mustn't let him make you into a puppet, Dana. He can do that, I've watched him."

"I won't. But he does pay my salary, and his track record with his nurses isn't super, I'm told." She lifted an eyebrow. "If he throws me out, who'll be brave enough to take my place?"

He winced. "What a horrible thought. Mother told me she begged your supervisor not to tell you everything about Gannon. She was afraid you wouldn't come."

Dana laughed. "I might not have. But once I got here, I wouldn't have left for the world. He challenged me, you see."

"If you want a real challenge," he said dryly, "you ought to wander into his study right now. I barely escaped with my skin intact."

"What did you do to irritate him?" she asked.

He chuckled, watching the ocean begin to darken as the sun set. "I breathed," he murmured. "He's thumping around the room, knocking over furniture and cursing everything from the color of the sky to the carpet that keeps tripping him up."

She drew in a slow breath. "Should I go in and see if I can calm him before your mother jumps off the balcony?"

"I see you've figured Lorraine out very well," he observed. "She's very nervous when he's in a temper—and he hasn't been any other way since the accident."

"At least you believe as the doctors and I do: that it's all a matter of making him realize he hasn't lost his sight permanently."

"Oh, I agree, all right. But Gannon's the one who has to be convinced. And, lady," he added with a grin, "that is going to be a full-time job, and not without hazards."

"I've already found that out," she said with a sigh.

"Won't you change your mind and come with me?"

She looked up at him thoughtfully. "If you'll take Mr. van der Vere along, too, I'll come."

He lifted his eyes helplessly to the sky. "What a horrible thought."

"Will you?"

He looked down, his head cocked, his eyes twinkling. "For you, lovely lady, anything."

"Not so lovely," she murmured, touching the scar.

"It hardly shows," he argued. "And it's healing. You'll be left with hardly a memory of it in a few weeks."

"I suppose."

"Is that why you came here?" he asked quietly, stopping to watch her expression. "To hide your scars?"

She stared at the sand under her own bare feet. "I suppose I did, in a way. My mother died in an accident a few months ago, you see. She'd been drinking, and I let her drive. . . ." Her shoulders lifted and fell. "I got a few scars and I had a concussion, but everyone seems to feel that I killed her."

"Do they?" he asked thoughtfully, "or is it guilt that's punishing you?"

Her eyes flashed. "Guilt?"

"Your eyes are tortured, Miss Steele," he said softly, studying them. "You're very young to try to live with that much guilt. I'm a fatalist myself. I believe that the hour of death is preordained."

She swallowed. "Is it?"

"Such things are best left to theologians and philosophers. But it seems to me a horrible waste to let guilt destroy your life along with your mother's. Was she a happy person?"

She shook her head. "My parents had divorced, my father had remarried and Mandy found it rough trying to live by herself." She stuck her hands in her pockets. "She couldn't cope. She wanted me to come back home, to take care of her." She laughed bitterly. "I couldn't even take care of myself. . . ."

He caught her gently by the shoulders and turned her to face him. "Try living in the present. You can't change what was."

She felt her lower lip tremble. "The guilt is eating me alive."

"Then stop feeding it," he advised. "Stop hiding."

She searched his kind eyes. "Have you ever thought of becoming a psychiatrist?" she asked, forcing lightness into her tone.

One corner of his mouth curled up. "I studied psychology for three years before I decided I liked electronics better and transferred to a technical college," he confessed.

She burst out laughing. "I should have realized," she said. "You could probably do your brother more good than I have, you know."

"He won't listen to me or talk to me," he said, shaking his head. "But he'll listen to you."

"Only when I yell."

"It's a start. You really want to take him to Savannah? Okay. But you tell him. I'm not going back in there to save my life," he chuckled.

"I find that blatant cowardice," she murmured.

"No doubt. I call it self-preservation." He strode back down the beach beside her. "Have you told him—about the scars?"

"No," she said simply. She swallowed. "You . . . won't tell him?"

He glanced at her. "You're making too much of them, you know," he said softly. "You're a lovely woman. But if you don't want him to know . . ."

"It's not for any special reason," she said quickly. "It's just that, well, he doesn't need to know, does he?"

He turned away before she could see the tiny smile on his face. "No, of course he doesn't."

They walked quietly back to the house, and Dana gathered all her nerve before she knocked at the door of Gannon's study.

"Come in" was the harsh reply.

She opened the door, to find him sitting in his big armchair with tumbled furniture all around him, a black scowl on his face and a smoking cigarette in his hand.

"Who is it?" he asked shortly.

"It's me," Dana said.

The scowl blackened. "Back from your daily constitutional?" he asked sarcastically. "Did my brother go with you?"

"Yes, he did," she said coolly. "It was quite a nice change, to walk and talk without yelling."

He snorted, taking another draw from the cigarette. "Can you find me an ashtray?"

"Why?" she asked innocently, noting the pile of ashes beside the chair on the carpet. "Are you tired of dumping them on the floor already?"

"Don't get cute. Just find me an ashtray and bring it here."

She didn't like the silky note in his voice, but she got the ashtray and approached him warily.

"Where are you?" he asked, cocking his head and listening intently.

She set the ashtray softly on the arm of the chair and moved back. "Back here," she replied then. "Your ashtray is next to you."

He muttered something. "Afraid to come too close? Wise woman."

She shifted from one foot to the other. "It's my time off," she reminded him, "but I wanted to ask you something."

"I know it's your time off," he said curtly. "You remind me every day exactly how much you have and when you want it, so why the poor little slave girl act over the supper table? Playing on Dirk's sympathies? I might warn you that my brother is something of a playboy: He likes skirts."

"He's a nice, kind man, and you ought to be half as blessed with his good humor," she threw back.

"Shrew!" he accused, sitting up straight. His face hardened; his eyes darkened. "If I could see you, you'd be in considerable trouble right now."

"What would you do, take me over your knee?" she asked.

His nostrils flared. "No, I wouldn't risk breaking my hand."

"How discerning of you," she murmured.

His eyes searched in her direction, and something wicked flared in them. "I think I'd rather kiss you speechless than hit you."

She couldn't help it. She flushed like a budding rose, gaping at him. Her knees felt strangely weak as the words brought back vivid memories.

"No comment?" he murmured. "Have I shocked you? Or would you rather forget that last night in my arms you responded like a woman instead of a shrew?"

"I'm your nurse, Mr. van der Vere, not. . . !" she began.

"You're a woman," he interrupted, "and somehow I think that fact has escaped you for a long time. You have the feel of fine porcelain, as if you've never been touched by human hands. Is it part of the shield you wear to keep the world at bay? Are you afraid of feeling too much?"

"I'm afraid of being accused of unethical conduct," she returned. "You aren't the first man who's made a pass at me, Mr. van der Vere, and, sadly, you probably won't be the last. Sick men do sometimes make a grab for their nurses if the nurses are young and not too unattractive."

"The unattractive bit wouldn't matter to a blind man, would it?" he asked shortly.

"The blindness is temporary," she said firmly. "The doctors have told you that. Your sight will return; there's no tissue damage—"

He cursed roundly. "There is!" he shot back. He got to his feet and almost fell in his haste.

She rushed forward without thinking and helped him regain his balance, only to find herself trapped in his arms before she could move away.

"Mr. van der Vere," she said with controlled firmness, "please let me go."

But his fingers tightened, and a look of sudden pain washed over his features as her small hands pressed helplessly against his warm, broad chest. "Dana, don't push me away," he said softly.

The quiet plea took the fight out of her. She stared up at him, hating what he made her feel, hating her own reaction to it. But how could she fight him like this?

His big hands ran up and down her arms. "I wish I could see you," he said harshly.

"There's nothing uncommon about me. I'm just an ordinary woman," she said quietly. "I'm not a beauty; I'm plain."

"Let me find that out for myself," he said, letting his hands move to the sides of her face. "Let me feel you."

"No!" She tried to move away, but his hands were too strong.

"What is there about my touch that frightens you?" he asked harshly. "I won't hurt you, I promise."

"It isn't that. . . !"

"Then, what?" His face contorted. "For God's sake, am I such a leper? Does my blindness repel you. . . ?"

Her eyes closed; her lower lip trembled. There was nothing for it now: She was going to have to tell him the truth or let him feel it, and she didn't think she could bear that. She didn't want him to know that she was disfigured.

"I'm . . . there's a scar," she whispered shakily, her eyes closed so that she missed the expression on his face. "Down my left cheek. A very long one."

His hands shifted, and he found the scar with its puckered surface and traced it from her temple down past her ear, traced it with fingers that suddenly trembled.

Her eyes closed even more tightly. "I didn't want you to know," she whispered.

"Dana." He searched her delicate features with warm, slow fingers, tracing her eyebrows, her eyes, her nose, her cheeks and, finally, her trembling mouth.

"It's like a bow, isn't it?" he whispered, drawing his forefinger over the line of her mouth. "Do you wear lipstick?"

"No," she admitted. "I . . . I don't like it."

"Firm little chin, high cheekbones, wide-spaced eyes . . . and a scar that I can barely feel, which must hardly show at all." He bent and brushed his mouth over the scar with such tenderness that her eyes clouded and tears escaped from them.

"Don't cry," he whispered.

She swallowed. "You make it seem so . . . so small a thing."

"It is. Beauty is more than skin deep—isn't that what they say? You have a lovely young soul . . . and a stubborn spirit that makes me gnash my teeth, even though I respect it." He lifted his head. "Dana, I'd give a lot to taste your mouth again. But that wouldn't be ethical, I suppose, and we must above all be ethical."

She smiled at his cynicism. "Yes, we must," she murmured. She disentangled herself gently from his hands and he let her go with a sigh. "Now, about going to Savannah . . ."

His face darkened and he scowled. "I do not want you to go. . . ."

"Oh, Dirk and I aren't going alone," she assured him. "We're taking you with us."

He blinked. "What?"

"We thought the ride would do you good," she murmured. "Help your disposition, as it were. Blow the cobwebs away."

He chuckled softly, then loudly, and she loved the masculine beauty of his face when it relaxed. "I can think of something that would do my disposition a lot more good than a drive," he murmured, tongue in cheek.

She cleared her throat and moved toward the door. "You just sit here and think about that. I'm going."

"Coward," he said silkily.

"Strategic retreat," she corrected. She paused at the doorway. "Thank you for what you said about the scar, Mr. van der Vere."

"My name is Gannon," he reminded her. "I'd . . . like to hear you say it."

"Gannon," she whispered, making a caress of it. She turned away from his set features. "Good night."

She barely heard his own "Good night" as the door closed behind her.

Chapter Six

Dana had never seen a city like Savannah, having spent most of her life around Ashton. She was overwhelmed by the history of the sprawling city, and when she and Dirk and Gannon had lunch at an eighteenth-century pirate inn, she almost swooned.

"Pirates really stopped here?" she asked in a whisper, staring around at the homey interior, which was crowded with lunch guests.

"According to legend, they did," Gannon murmured. "If I remember correctly, you can see the ocean from the window, can you not?"

She glanced out toward the horizon. "Oh, yes, you certainly can. What kinds of boats are those way out there?"

"Take your pick—shrimp boats, fishing boats, trawlers, tugboats. . . . It's a busy harbor," Dirk commented. "The seafood here is super."

"Something else we need to show her," Gannon said between sips of his hot, creamy coffee, "is one of the hidden gardens."

A flower-lover, her ears perked up. "Hidden gardens?"

"Little courtyards. Most of them are in private homes, but we have cousins here who love visitors. We'll drive by before we leave the city," Gannon told her. "I think you'll be impressed."

"I'm glad we didn't bring Lorraine." Dirk chuckled. "Every time she visits Maude and Katy, she wants to renovate the beach house."

"Maude and Katy are spinsters," Gannon continued. "Maude married, but her husband is dead, so she lives with Katy, who never married. They're sisters."

"You'll like the furniture especially, I think," Dirk added. "Most of it is mahogany. It came from the West Indies, where one of our ancestors made a fortune in shipping."

"Indeed he did," Gannon chuckled. "Raiding British ships. He was a pirate."

"Now I know why Gannon's so hard to get along with," Dana told Dirk with a wicked grin. "It's in his blood. I wonder how many people that pirate ancestor tossed overboard to feed hungry sharks?"

"Only one, as legends go," Gannon said, his eyes twinkling as they stared straight ahead. "His wife," he added on a low chuckle.

"Well, the old blackguard!" Dana exclaimed.

"He found her in his cabin with his first mate,"

he whispered, "and tied them together and pushed them from the starboard deck into the ocean."

She shivered. "What happened to him?"

"Nobody's sure," Gannon continued. "But at least one legend says that he went on to become a provincial governor in the West Indies."

"Injustice," Dana grumbled.

"That depends on your definition," Gannon reminded her. "Those were different times; there were different codes of honor. In those days it was suicide for a woman to be adulterous."

"And these days it's more the 'in' thing than not," Dirk nodded. "How times change."

"Not always for the better," Dana added. Her eyes widened as she saw the platters of seafood being brought by their waitress. "Food!" she exclaimed.

"I hope your appetite is up to it," Dirk teased.

"If it isn't, I'll go home with my pockets full," she returned, and was pleased to hear Gannon's laughter mingling with his brother's.

The happy mood lasted and seemed to increase when they reached the Victorian home of the sisters Van Bloom. Maude was tall and thin and Katy was short and dumpy, but they shared a love of people that went beyond their physical attributes.

Dana was amazed at the garden she saw when she walked through the black wrought-iron gate. The courtyard was floored with brick, and its size was about that of a medium-size living room. It was filled with flowers and potted shrubs and trees, and there was black wrought-iron furniture set near a small fountain positioned in front of a vine-covered wall. Dana could understand why Lorraine felt like redoing the beach house every time she came to the Van Blooms'. It made the most infrequent gardener's fingers itch to recreate it.

"Lovely, isn't it?" Gannon said from behind her. "I remember it very well."

"You may have appreciated it, my dear," Maude said shortly, "but that woman you brought with you last time most certainly did not. Did you hear her, muttering about putting in a bar and a hot tub. . . !"

Dana turned, frowning, and Gannon looked distinctly uncomfortable.

"Layn likes modern surroundings, Aunt," Gannon said curtly. "What kinds of flowers do you have in here?"

Maude hesitated before she let the subject of Gannon's former girl friend drop. "Azaleas, my dear," she said. "Roses and sultanas and geraniums in shades of pink and red. I particularly like the red. How about you, Miss Steele?"

Dana sighed. "Oh, I just love them all," she said with quiet enthusiasm. "I don't think I've ever seen anything so lovely."

"You might try one of your own; it isn't so difficult," Maude encouraged.

"The nurse's home isn't the best place, I'm afraid," Dana said wryly.

"You're a nurse?" Maude burst out. "Why, so am I. I practiced as an R.N. for over fifteen years before I retired. Come, my dear, let's sit and discuss the changes over a pot of hot tea."

It was a long time before the two women finished, and then suddenly the others had joined them and it was time to leave. Dana climbed into the front seat with Dirk, while Gannon sat alone and quiet in the backseat and turned his head in the direction of the charming old home with a feeling of loss.

"Isn't it grand?" Dana sighed. "Are there many of those courtyards in Savannah?"

"More than you'd imagine," Dirk replied. "There's an active historical foundation here, with conscientious members who have a love of history and a sense of continuity. They've accomplished a lot, as you'll notice when we go through the downtown area. General Oglethorpe planned for gardens when he laid out the grid pattern of the first streets in the city, you see. He even established a sort of public nursery. Savannah is famous for its public squares as well."

"It's a beautiful city. I wish we had more time to see it," Dana said.

"We'll come back again," Dirk promised with a grin. "You're the kind of girl I like to take sightseeing, Dana: You have such a natural enthusiasm for new things."

"I love beauty, that's all," she replied. "Thank you for today, Dirk."

"Today will be the first of many," the younger man promised. "We'll do this again."

In the backseat, Gannon's face grew darker and harder, and neither of the occupants of the front seat noticed that he wasn't taking part in the conversation. Dana was lost in the memory of what she'd seen, and Dirk was capitalizing on her interest to freeze his brother out of the running. He liked what he saw in this soft-voiced wildflower, and he wasn't planning to lose her to his freebooter of a brother. He was going to stake a claim while there was still time.

Dana, blissfully unaware of her companion's dark thoughts, was chattering away about the garden without a care in the world. The gaiety lasted until they were back at the beach house and inside, until Gannon called sharply for her to join him in the study. And when the door closed, the beauty of the day went into a total eclipse with his harsh outburst.

"Your job," he said without preamble, standing rigidly in the middle of the floor, "is to look after me, not to flirt with my brother."

She froze at the door, staggered by the attack. "I beg your pardon?"

"You heard me," he growled. "From now on there'll be no more of that. While you work for me, you do it exclusively. I will not have my routine interrupted by these charming little outings with Dirk."

"You came too," she burst out. "And I'll remind you that you only pay for my services, not my soul!"

"That," he said, "is debatable. Keep away from Dirk."

She drew herself up to her full height. "I will not," she said shortly. "As long as he's here I will show him the same politeness and courtesy that I show your mother. And if you don't like that, fire me."

"With pleasure. Pack your things and get out."

She hadn't been prepared for that. Wild thoughts whirled through her mind, the foremost among them being that she'd have to leave him, just when she was getting . . . used to him. But his face was as dark as thunder, and he had a look of a man who wouldn't back down half an inch to save his life.

"If that's what you want, Mr. van der Vere, I'll be pleased to leave you alone with your bad temper." She watched his rigid face twitch, as if her ready reply had come as a surprise. She could hardly resist a faint smile as she opened the door and went out. She'd had the last word, at least. But what would become of him now?

She started up the staircase when Lorraine appeared at the top of it.

"There you are," the older woman said with a smile. "What would you like for dinner? I've had the cook thaw some steaks—"

"I don't think I'll have time," Dana said quietly. "I'm going up to pack."

Lorraine paled. "But, my dear, you're doing so well with him. Won't you reconsider?"

"It's not me," Dana replied with a quiet smile. "I'd have stuck it out, but he just fired me."

The other woman blinked. "Fired you? Why?"

"I was flirting outrageously with his brother," was the amused reply. "Or so he said. I didn't know I had it in me."

Lorraine laughed softly. "Oh, my. It's not funny in the least, and I'm not laughing at you. But considering the length of time you've known my other stepson . . . Poor Gannon."

"Poor me," Dirk said from behind Dana. "I gather that something's afoot. Dana's been fired, and I'm the culprit?"

"I was flirting with you," Dana told him.

His eyebrows arched. "Were you? You might have told me about it; I didn't even notice."

"Dirk, do something," Lorraine pleaded. "Gannon simply can't fire Dana just when I've gotten used to her!"

"I'll see what I can do," Dirk sighed, giving the study door a long, hesitant glance. "But don't expect miracles."

"I, for one, will not. I'm packing." Dana started up the stairs. "Don't worry, Mrs. van der Vere, I'll find you someone tough to replace me—perhaps Mrs. Pibbs . . . ?"

"I was thinking more along the lines of that big man on that adventure show I like on television"—Lorraine scowled—"The one who hires himself out as a bouncer in his spare time. . . ."

Dana laughed softly. "Good luck." She went on up the stairs and into her room, closing the door gently behind her. It was just beginning to sink in that she didn't have a job or a place to go. Her job at the hospital had been filled of necessity, and without it she couldn't move back in with her roommate. She'd just joined the unemployed of the world, and all because her employer had some strange idea that she'd been making a play for his brother.

The more she thought about it, the madder she got. How dare he accuse her of chasing Dirk? It was just as well that she was leaving. Let him sit here and stew all alone; it seemed to be all he wanted from life. Let him wallow in self-pity and convince himself that he was blind forever, and see if she cared.

The problem was that she did care—very much. The thought of the big man sitting alone in that room without trying to help himself made her want to cry. Nobody else would last with him. And most nurses would just throw up their hands and walk out: They wouldn't take the kind of abuse he handed out. She didn't like to think of strangers doing the things for him that she did; even handing him his medicine and leading him around obstacles had become a part of her life that she didn't want to surrender.

And she would keep remembering the way he'd kissed her. . . . It had been unethical, but so sweet. She'd felt necessary for the first time in her life—secure and protected and needed. All the color would go out of the world when she left this lonely house by the sea.

She started packing her few things with a heart that felt like lead. The sudden tap on her door interrupted her, and she went to answer it with a thudding pulse.

Dirk was standing just outside, his hands in his pockets and a disgusted look on his face.

"I'm afraid I made it worse," he said apologetically, with a faint smile. "Not only wouldn't he relent, he went right through the ceiling and ordered me out of the house."

She sighed. She'd hoped . . . but what did it matter now? She returned the smile halfheartedly. "I'm sorry about that. He's in a nasty mood. I only wish I knew what was wrong with him."

"Are you quite sure you don't?" he asked with quiet suspicion. "He's very possessive about you. I haven't seen him this way since his early days with Layn, before he found out what a barracuda she really was."

Dana felt the blush work its way up into her hairline, and the fact that Dirk grinned wickedly didn't help it to fade.

"So it's like that," he murmured. "No wonder he was so angry when you decided to go to Savannah with me."

"It's not like that," she argued. "I'm his nurse. There is such a thing as ethics—"

"And such a thing as love," he interrupted. "What does ethics have to do with that? He cares for you—surely you've noticed it?"

Her eyes closed briefly. "I've noticed that he's . . . attached to me," she corrected. "But you must remember that he's blind—temporarily or not. It makes him feel vulnerable, and he doesn't like it. What he thinks he feels for me may be nothing more than affection. I'm his anchor right now. If he regains his sight—and I'm convinced that he will—I will no more fit into his world than he will fit into mine."

"That might have been true once," Dirk agreed, "but he's changing."

That was true, he was, even if just faintly. But Dana was too wary to hope, and she said so.

"I still think that if you went downstairs and talked to him yourself, you might change his mind," he added.

She laughed softly. "I don't agree. And pride is my greatest fault; I'm not easily bent, you see." She shrugged her slender shoulders. "It's better this way. Mrs. van der Vere won't find it very difficult to replace me. . . ."

"And you won't have risked an involvement, right?" he asked softly. "All right, it's your life. But I think you're making a big mistake."

"As you said," she reminded him quietly, "it is my life."

He nodded. "Well, take care of yourself. Although it's been brief, it's been nice knowing you. We may meet again someday."

She smiled. "It isn't likely. But thank you anyway. Good-bye."

"Good-bye."

She closed the door gently behind her and hated the quick tears that rushed into her eyes. She hadn't wanted to face what she was beginning to feel for Gannon van der Vere, but Dirk had forced her to. Yes, it was a good thing that it would end there. Because when Gannon did regain his sight, the last thing he'd want or need in his life would be a quiet, scared little nurse with inhibitions. And she was wise enough to realize it.

All the same, she paced the floor for what seemed like hours after she'd bathed and dressed for bed and finished gathering all her belongings into her suitcase. Her eyes felt bloodshot; her heart felt sore, as if wounded. She knew it was pointless to go to bed; she couldn't have slept.

The soft knock at the door seemed like a figment of her imagination, and she walked toward it like a daydreamer. Surely Dirk hadn't come back to say good-bye again?

She caught the doorknob, turned it and found a taciturn, weary-eyed Gannon standing quietly in the hall. He was wearing wine-colored pajamas with a long matching robe, and his blond hair was badly rumpled, as if he'd tried desperately to sleep and couldn't.

"Dana?" he asked softly

Her heart jumped wildly at the sound of her name. "Yes?" she said in a taut tone.

He jammed his big hands into his pockets and leaned wearily against the wall, his eyes staring straight ahead. "Do you want to go?"

"Throwing the ball back into my court?" she

mused. "Will it salve your pride if you can make me admit that I don't?"

He shook his head. "But it might make it easier for me to sleep. I . . . don't want to have to break in a new nurse now. I've gotten used to you. Warts and all," he added coolly.

It was insane, she told herself, to let herself be talked into staying. It would be better for both of them if she folded her tent and stole quietly away into his memory. But she looked at him and loved him; it was as simple as that. And the thought of leaving him became a nightmare.

"I'll only stay," she said firmly, "if you'll stop accusing me of things I haven't done with men I barely know."

His jaw tautened; his eyes flashed. But he sighed and nodded. "Very well. As long as you don't contemplate doing them," he agreed.

"If you could see me," she murmured, "just the thought of my flirting with a man would amuse you. I'm not even pretty."

"You have a lovely voice," he said, catching her by surprise. His fingers reached out and instinctively found her face, brushing lightly across her cheek and into her soft hair. His eyes closed in a scowl. "Don't go, Dana. You'd take the color with you."

"You'd very soon find someone to put it back," she told him, moving away from the disturbing feel of his fingers. "But if you like, I'll stay . . . a little longer."

He grinned then, and all the lines seemed to fall out of his hard face. "Until I fire you again?"

She smiled. "Until you fire me again."

"Get up early," he said, moving away from the wall. "I find myself looking forward to those walks along the beach with you."

"Yes . . . Gannon," she whispered, watching his face change, soften, mellow.

He nodded. "Yes. That's a start, at least. Good night, Dana."

"Good night."

He touched the wall until he reached his own room, and disappeared into the darkness. Dana stared after him quietly, surprised at the burst of joy she felt over what had happened. She didn't have to leave him. She stepped back into her own room with a silent prayer of thanks. At least she had his company for a little longer. She'd live on it all her life.

He was scowling when she appeared downstairs for breakfast the next morning, and Lorraine looked just as uncomfortable.

"Good morning, dear," she told Dana absently, chewing on her lower lip as she turned back to Gannon. "Are they sure? They could be mistaken again, since . . ."

"He said they aren't," he growled. He muttered a rough word under his breath and gripped his cup tightly in both hands. "I told you," he said shortly. "I knew from the beginning that hysteria wouldn't cause so much pain. They'll find it now, too, since they've discovered what I knew all along."

"What is it?" Dana asked quickly, sensing disaster.

Lorraine sighed. "The X rays—there was a mixup: One of the new people at the hospital mistook Gannon's for another patient and mislabeled them. It wasn't really her fault; she was certain that someone else had made the mistake and was trying to correct it."

Dana felt her face whiten. Gannon was sitting very straight, quietly sipping his coffee.

"There was something on the X rays they'd wrongly linked to another patient," Lorraine finished wearily. "When they did a brain scan, it came back clear, so they repeated the X rays. That was when they discovered it. It's been weeks, you see, and they'd told the other patient that nothing could be done." She shrugged. "Oddly enough, his sight came back. . . . It was only in one eye and was apparently truly hysterical in nature."

"Which mine isn't, apparently," Gannon growled. He set the coffee cup down so roughly that it sloshed everywhere, burning him.

Dana jumped up to dab at it and he pushed at her roughly.

She fell against the table with a gasp, and at the tiny sound he seemed to calm all at once.

"Dana?" He reached out. "Dana, did I hurt you? Dana!"

She rubbed her side. "I'm all right," she said quickly, shaking her head at Lorraine, who was rushing toward her. "I'm all right."

He moved closer, his whole look one of abject apology. "I'm sorry. I didn't mean to hurt you."

"You didn't. I collided with you, that's all." She

let him find her hand and clasp it warmly. Surges of pure pleasure shot up her arm at his touch. "I'm really fine."

He drew in a steadying breath. "Come down to the hospital with us, will you?" he asked. "I need you."

No three words had ever sounded quite so sweet to her. "Of course I will," she said. "I'll be here as long as you need me."

Lorraine went to get her car keys, looking oddly relieved.

The next few hours seemed to drag on forever, and Dana felt cold fear eating away at her as Gannon went through test after test. Lorraine paced and muttered and looked increasingly more concerned.

Finally they were called into Dr. Shane's office, where the rotund little physician stated the evidence of the tests bluntly and without pulling his punches.

"It's shrapnel," he said quietly, watching Gannon start. "Apparently from the accident—a tiny sliver that lodged itself in the brain, affecting the optic nerve."

"Can you operate?" Gannon asked curtly.

"No."

Dana's eyes closed, hurting for him, because now it was permanent and now he knew it. She was already going over it in her mind before Dr. Shane continued, having seen that type of injury in war patients.

"The only chance you have to regain your sight,"

the doctor told Gannon, "is if the shrapnel should shift again. And it isn't completely impossible, you know. A sneeze is violent enough to dislodge it, although it isn't likely to. I'm afraid that's all the hope I can give you. If we were to try to operate, we could do irreparable damage to your brain. It's far too delicate and too great a risk. I'm very sorry about the mixup in the X rays, Gannon, but it would have made no difference if it hadn't happened. The condition is inoperable."

Gannon stood up quietly and held out his hand, shaking the doctor's. "Thank you for being honest with me. As you see," he added ironically, "I was right all along."

"Fortunately you have a nurse to help you cope," Dr. Shane reminded him, "and a computer company to provide you with excellent assistance in those new techniques that help the blind communicate with the outside world. You'll do well."

"Yes," Gannon said. "I'll do well."

He was putting on a great front. He looked like a man without a care in the world, but Dana didn't believe it, and neither did Lorraine.

"Stay with him," she pleaded, drawing Dana aside when they got back to the beach house. "I'm afraid for him. He's taking it far too calmly to suit me, and you're the only person he's going to allow very close to him."

"I'll take care of him," Dana promised. She touched Lorraine's arm. "Please don't worry. I'll take care of him."

"Yes, dear, I know you will." She smiled sadly. "It's in your eyes whenever you look at him. But don't let him hurt you, Dana."

"I haven't that choice anymore," she admitted softly, smiling before she turned and went into the study with him and closed the door.

"Would you like something to eat?" she asked when he stood out on the balcony, listening to the waves crash against the shore.

He shook his head. Behind him his hands were clasped so tightly that they looked white in spite of their tan.

"Can I do anything for you?" she persisted.

He drew in a deep, slow breath. "Yes. Come here and let me hold you."

Denying him was the last thought in her mind. She went to him as if she had no other function in life but to do and be anything he wanted of her.

He found her shoulders and pulled her close, wrapping her against his big, taut body. His body suddenly convulsed, and he buried his face in the long strands of loosened hair at her throat.

"Oh, God, I'm blind," he ground out harshly, and his body shuddered once heavily as the emotion poured out of him. "Blind! I knew it, I knew. . . . Dana, what will I do? How will I live? I'd rather be dead. . . !"

"No!" She pressed closer, holding him, her hands soothing, her cheek nuzzling against him, her voice firm and quiet. "No, you mustn't talk that way. You learned to cope before; you can again.

You can get used to it. I'll help you cope, I will. I'll never leave you, Gannon, never, never!" she whispered.

He rocked her against him, and she felt something suspiciously wet against her throat where his hot face was pressed. "Promise me," he ground out. "Swear to me that you won't leave me unless I send you away. Promise!"

It sounded very much like an ultimatum, and she was afraid of what he might do if she refused or argued with him. "Yes, I promise," she agreed softly. Her eyes closed and she savored the feel of him against her, the warmth of his body comforting, like the crush of his big arms. "I promise."

He seemed to slump in relief, and his fingers against her back soothed, idly caressing. "It was a blow," he confessed softly. "I had expected . . . I had expected them to find something operable, you see. I wanted a miracle."

"Miracles happen every day when people still believe in them," she reminded him. "You're still alive; isn't that a miracle in itself? You're big and healthy and you have everything in the world to live for."

"Everything except my sight," he said shortly.

"I'll remind you that there are many people in the world without sight who have accomplished quite a lot despite it," she said. "Singers, artists, musicians, scientists . . . nothing is a handicap unless you force it to be. You can accomplish anything you want to."

"Even marriage?" he scoffed, lifting his head. A family?"

"That as well."

"And who would marry the blind man, Nurse? You?" he laughed, and his smile was cruel; his hands on her arms bit in painfully. "Would you marry a blind man?"

"Yes," she said with her whole heart, loving every line of his face, oblivious to what was happening, even to the words themselves as she drowned in the joy of being near him.

He blinked, and the hardness drained out of his face. "You would . . . marry me, Dana?" he whispered.

"Any woman . . ."

"You," he corrected curtly. He shook her gently. "Would you marry me, blind?"

"Gannon, if it's a rhetorical question . . ." she began unsteadily.

"Will you marry me, Dana?" he persisted, making each word clear and strong. His face hardened. "No more red herrings; just answer me, will you?"

"But do be sensible; we don't love each other," she pleaded.

"You love me," he corrected, smiling when she stiffened. "Oh, yes, it stands out a mile, even to an inexperienced man, and I'm not that. I know how you feel. You sound and smell and feel like a woman in love, and when I touch you this way, you melt against me. Professional compassion? No, Dana, it isn't that. Now is it?"

She swallowed, her lips parting. "It's . . . infatuation," she whispered. "You're so alien from any man I've ever known, and I know nothing of men. Is it surprising?"

He shook his head. "Not at all, but I'm going to take shameless advantage of it. Marry me, Dana. I can't promise you undying love, but I'll take care of you; I'll be good to you. And all you'll have to do in return is lead me around and keep me from blowing out my brains. . . ."

"Stop it!" She pressed her hand frantically against his warm, hard lips and trembled when they pressed back into its palm.

"Would you care that much?" he laughed. "You don't even want my money, do you, little one? That in itself makes you an oddity in my world. Take a chance, Dana—say yes. I'll make it good for you, in every way there is."

She wanted to. She needed to. But it wasn't possible, and she knew that too.

"I can't," she whispered miserably.

He stiffened. "Why not?"

"Because there's every possibility that someday you'll regain your sight—the doctor told you as much—and what if you did and found yourself tied to someone like me?" she ground out. "You'd be ashamed—"

He stopped the tirade with his lips. She went taut under the hard, demanding pressure, feeling something unleashed in him that had been carefully controlled up until now. She pushed against his broad chest, but he wouldn't relent, not an inch.

"Ashamed of you?" he growled at her lips. "Never! Now, stop talking nonsense and kiss me back. We're going to be husband and wife, so you'd better learn to like this with me. We're going to do quite a lot of it through the years ahead. Come on, don't turn away. Kiss me."

"I won't marry you, I won't," she protested.

"Then we'll be engaged until I can make you change your mind," he murmured, brushing his lips maddeningly over hers, feeling the helpless trembling of her mouth at the newness of the caress. His hands dropped to her waist and brought her gently against him. "Just engaged," he whispered. "All right, butterfly? I won't even rush you to the altar. Just agree to that much and I'll stop talking about leaping onto the rocks. . . ."

She shuddered at the thought of his body bruised and broken by those huge boulders. "Gannon . . ."

"Say yes," he whispered. His mouth bit at hers—warm, slow kisses that drugged her, that drained her of protest.

She reached up to hold his warm face between her hands, giving in to a pleasure she'd never known. "I shouldn't," she told him.

"But you're going to," he murmured, smiling. "Sweet little mouth, it tastes of honey, did you know? Now, stop talking and kiss me better. I've had a terrible morning. Make it better for me, can't you?"

She wanted to say no, she wanted to ignore the proposal, she wanted to run. But she heard her own breathless voice agreeing with him, felt her body lifting against the crush of his arms, felt herself go under in a maze of sweet magic as he kissed her long and tenderly. And then Lorraine was suddenly in the room, offering congratulations, and it was too late to protest, to take it back. Before she could open her mouth to deny it, she was drinking champagne as Gannon van der Vere's new fiancée.

Chapter Seven

Once Gannon decided to come out of his shell and cope with the reality of his blindness, he seemed to change overnight. He called in one of his computer experts and they locked themselves away in his study for the better part of a day. When the caller left, Gannon was grinning from ear to ear.

"I'd love to know what's going on," Dana ventured as she joined him, closing the door gently behind her.

"Progress," he said. He lifted his head. "Where are you? Come here."

She went to him as naturally as if she were walking into a room, feeling his big arm draw her close to his side with wonder.

"Did it happen?" he asked, his voice mirroring

the same uncertainty she felt. "Did you really agree to marry me?"

She sighed and leaned her head against his shoulder. "I was out of my mind," she confessed. "I should have said no. You'll regret it. . . ."

"Never!" He turned her into his arms and stood holding her tightly, his breath warm and soft at her ear. "Never, not as long as I live. We'll have a good life together." He found her chin and lifted it. "Dana, you meant it? You do love me?"

She swallowed. Where was her pride, her caution? He'd as much as admitted that he didn't love her, that all he could offer her was companionship.

"Yes," she said anyway, studying the lines and angles of his face with soft, loving eyes. "Oh, yes, I meant it, Gannon."

His chiseled lips parted on a heavy breath and he seemed troubled. His hands moved up to her soft arms and stroked them idly. "I feel as if I'm cheating you," he confessed. "Perhaps . . . perhaps we should call it off—now, while there's still time."

She understood. He was telling her that he could never love her. But she was willing to settle for what he could give; even the crumbs of his affection would be more than she'd ever had in her young, lonely life.

"I'm willing to take the chance—if you are," she said after a minute, and the strangest expression crossed his hard features.

"I'll take care of you," he told her. "That may sound ridiculous, coming from a blind man. But if you trust me with your future, I'll do everything in my power to see that you don't regret it."

She smiled. Hesitantly, shyly, she reached up to touch his face, her fingers cool and trembling where they brushed against his cheek.

He flinched, and she started to tug her hand back, but he caught it and pressed it firmly against the warm, slightly abrasive flesh of his face.

"No, don't draw back, Dana," he said on a whisper. "You startled me, that's all. I like to be touched by you."

"Your face is rough," she murmured, studying it. "You have to shave twice a day, don't you?"

He nodded, smiling. "You'll discover after we're married that I feel like a bear early in the morning."

She blushed to the roots of her hair, and her breath caught. He heard it, laughing delightedly.

"Oh, bright spirit," he breathed. "What did I do in my life to deserve something as untouched and untarnished as you?"

She felt tears warm her eyes at the unexpected words. "I'm only a woman," she reminded him.

He shook his head, and his eyes sought the sound of her voice. They were dark with emotion, narrow, as if he'd have given anything at that moment to be able to see her.

"No, you're something completely out of my experience," he corrected. "The women in my life have been hard and jaded. I never realized that fact until we met. I think you've spoiled me, Dana. I didn't know there were people like you left in the world. God knows, my world wasn't peopled with them."

"Your world sounded very superficial to me," she said quietly. "As if people walked around without really feeling deeply, or thinking deeply, or participating in life."

"That was so." His hands moved up her arms to find her face and cup it. "I had nothing and never knew it. You make even my darkness bearable, purposeful. I begin to understand what you said to me at the beginning about a life of service."

"You do?" she whispered.

"That man who just left? He was my computer expert. We are beginning research on a unit that will outperform our present equipment designed to assist the blind. It will be a unit that can convert the printed word into sound—that can read text to an unsighted person." He grinned delightedly. "The first of many innovations, I expect. I think that I have never felt such pleasure as I feel at this moment, not only because such a device will assist me, but because it will assist so many others like me."

She burst into tears. She couldn't help it. Such a statement, coming from the hard, cold man of her early days there, brought such joy that she couldn't contain it.

"Dana," he whispered, drawing her gently closer, rocking her. "Doesn't it please you to have reformed me?"

She could hardly speak at all, she was so choked

up. "Oh, yes, it pleases me," she said fervently. "Gannon, what a beautiful thing to do!"

"Contamination," he whispered wickedly. "Being around you is making a civilized man of me. How do you like that?"

"I like it very much," she replied, pressing closer.

"So do I," he murmured. His hands smoothed down her tumbled hair. "It is, at least, a beginning. For now, Pratt has left me a device that we marketed last year. Come, I'll show you how it works."

She dabbed at her red eyes, following him to the desk, where a computer was sitting, along with a printer.

He sat down in front of the machine, booted up the system and fed a disk into it. Immediately, a mechanical voice began reading to him what was obviously a marketing report. He leaned back in his chair, grinning in her direction.

"What do you think?" he asked, interrupting the program with a light touch on the keyboard. "It gives me access to any company information I might need, at the touch of a finger. Even the disks have been coded with raised letters so that I can choose those I need. This terminal"—he tapped it—"is connected to the main computer at my office. With it I can access any information I need to send information back. Memos, letters and such. I can even contact other computers with the serial interface and a telephone modem."

"Science fiction," she whispered, awed.

"The tip of the iceberg," he returned. "The computer revolution has done more for the visually and audially impaired than anything else to date. And this is the bare beginning. Within ten years the entire industry as we know it will be so improved that this machine will seem obsolete."

"But I thought your company specialized in electronic equipment?" she murmured, standing close.

"It did. Now it's going to specialize in sensory aid devices for the blind and deaf," he said firmly. "And the first order of business is going to be finding ways to cut costs and make that equipment easily affordable for the people who need it."

"Oh, Gannon," she whispered, choking.

"Come here, waterspout," he chuckled softly, drawing her down into his strong arms. "Don't cry all over me—you'll short-circuit my computer."

"I'll try," she promised, cuddling close. "Gannon, you're a nice man."

"I suppose I can get used to being called that," he sighed. "But bear with me, it's very new."

"Yes," she agreed, laughing softly at the newness of being in his arms. "It is."

"How about getting me a cup of coffee while I go through this report?" he asked. "As much as I hate having you out of my arms for that long . . ."

"I'll be right back," she promised, getting to her feet. She left him with the computer and walked dreamily into the kitchen to get his coffee.

Apparently his good humor even extended to

Dirk, because later that week he invited his brother down to help him work out some details on the new sensory equipment. Dana took the opportunity to go into town and shop, with Lorraine's guidance, for her wedding dress.

Dana's eye was caught by a striking brunette who was going through the boutique's collection of evening gowns, and she noticed Lorraine suddenly stiffening.

"Layn Dalmont!" the older woman gasped.

As if the tiny sound caught her attention, the willowy brunette turned, her dark eyes flashing as they recognized Gannon's stepmother. She smiled, her attention shifting indifferently to Dana.

"Well, well, look who's here!" Layn laughed, abandoning the dresses to float toward them, a vision in red chiffon.

"Hello, Layn," Lorraine said tautly.

"Hello, Lorraine. And who's this? The little fiancée I've heard about?" she added, giving Dana an amused scrutiny. "How fortunate for Gannon that he's blind, honey, or he wouldn't give you the time of day."

It was what Dana knew already, but it stung to hear it put into words. She lifted her small face and smiled back. "How nice to meet you, Layn," she said quietly. "I've heard all about you."

The other woman started, as if she hadn't expected such a polite reply, but she said nothing in return.

"How have you been, Layn?" Lorraine asked, also politely.

"Bored, darling" was the curt reply. "Life without Gannon is very dull. How is he, by the way? Still mourning me?"

"Hardly, when he's about to be married," the elderly woman said with sweet venom.

"On the rebound, no doubt," the willowy brunette said, with a cold smile at Dana.

"You're welcome to come to the ceremony," Dana invited, smiling back. "Any friend of Gannon's, as the saying goes . . ."

Layn cleared her throat. "I have other commitments. I'll be sure to send you a wedding present." Her cold eyes went to Dana's cheek. "Perhaps some veils. . . ?" She turned and strode away, leaving Lorraine gasping.

"Oh, that woman!" Gannon's stepmother burst out. "How cruel!"

"How true," Dana corrected, unruffled. "Please, don't let it upset you. She may be troubled by her own conscience, and I can take care of myself, you know."

Lorraine visibly relaxed. "Yes, I've noticed that. Even Gannon doesn't get the best of you, my dear." She laughed. "It was delightful to see that Layn didn't, either."

"I see what Dirk meant, though. She does remind me of a barracuda," she added unkindly, with a small laugh. "We'd better get home. I can shop for dresses another day, when the vibrations are a little less hostile. All right?"

"If you like, Dana. I'm sorry Layn spoiled this for you."

She shrugged. "I let her spoil it . Anyway, we haven't even set a date for the wedding yet, so it's no loss."

As they drove home, though, that realization began to bother her. Gannon hadn't liked to talk about actual dates, as if he were reluctant to set one. Perhaps he was no more sure of success than she was. Perhaps he really did miss Layn and regretted proposing to Dana. Layn was right about one thing: sighted, he'd never have preferred his plain little nurse to the other woman.

She steered away from the study when they got home and sought the solace of the beach instead. Her mind was troubled. Gannon had seemed to brood a great deal. Lately she hadn't been too concerned about that until that day—until she'd seen Layn. But what if he was regretting his hasty proposal? What if he'd only been searching for a way to keep Dana with him, and marriage was the only way he'd found?

He didn't act like a man in love; he'd admitted that he wasn't. He'd told her that he had nothing to offer except companionship, affection. Would that be enough to last them all their lives? What if he regained his sight? How would he react to being tied to a woman who paled when compared to his beautiful Layn?

She stood watching the waves crash onto the beach and she knew all at once that she couldn't go through with it. She couldn't marry him. But how was she going to go back into his study and tell him?

She'd have to leave. There was no choice about that. She'd have to go back to Ashton and find a job. She'd have to face her relatives. . . .

Oddly enough, the grief over her mother's death was subsiding in the wake of her problems here with Gannon. She still felt an ache, a cold place deep inside that held loss and grief. But it was all beginning to fall into place. She was coming to grips with her own guilt, with the blame she'd transferred to her father, to the overreaction to her aunt's tactless remark. She seemed to have gone a little mad after the accident and was just now putting the pieces of her mind back together. Going home was no longer the terror it had been.

But still there was the problem of Gannon, the unwanted task ahead of explaining to him why she couldn't go through with the wedding. And along with it was the prospect of living her whole life without him. She closed her eyes, burning up with the love she felt for the big, bad-tempered man. She'd never felt so secure and safe in her life as she had with him, needing nothing more than his company, the pleasure of looking at him, holding his hand. Living without him was going to be almost as bad as losing her mother. How was she going to bear it? And most of all, how was she going to tell him?

She heard her name being bellowed from the steps that led to the beach from the house, and she smiled at the familiar voice that was audible above the crashing surf.

Barefoot, she joined him, her hair loose, and as she caught sight of his calm, relaxed face all her good intentions deserted her. *Let tomorrow take care of itself,* she decided. It would, and God would guide her steps. He always had, after all.

"Dana!"

"I'm here," she said, moving close. "I was just walking."

He smiled. "Walk with me, then. I've had all I can take of business for one day." He held out his hand, and she took it, feeling secure and warm all over at just his touch.

"I thought you were going to catch up on all the loose ends," she murmured.

He chuckled, a relaxed sound that pleased her ears. "I had good intentions. The drawback to the audio devices are that they wear you out. A sighted person can look back over a page of figures, but I had to do it by listening. It gets very repetitious."

"The new devices are just the same, aren't they?" she asked.

"They are. It's one of the drawbacks. But it's the best thing we have, to date."

"That new aid you mentioned, the one that reads printed material—was it your company that developed it?" she asked.

"We were one of several companies to hit upon the technology together, although we weren't the first to produce and market it," he told her. He grinned. "What is it they say, Dana, about great minds running in the same direction?"

She laughed with him, leaning companionably against his arm as they walked. He was so tremendous, so good to lean against, to depend on.

"Did you find your wedding gown?" he asked after a minute.

The question brought back unpleasant memories. "Not yet," she said quietly. "I'll go and look some more another day."

He scowled in her direction. "What happened?" he asked curtly, immediately certain that something was wrong. "Come on, don't hedge. What happened?"

"We . . . we saw Layn Dalmont at the shop," she said after a minute.

He stiffened, as if he'd been slapped. "Did you?"

His own posture betrayed him, and she turned away to stick her hands in the pockets of her jeans while she watched the ocean. "She's very lovely," she said.

"Yes, she is." His head was cocked to one side, his arms folded across his massive chest. "What did she say to you?"

"Very little," she replied honestly. "Mostly that she was bored to death without you."

He smiled faintly. "I'm not surprised. I spent a lot of money keeping her happy."

Her eyes closed, and she was glad that he couldn't see her face. "Lorraine told her that we were getting married."

That brought his head up attentively. "Did she? What did she say?"

Dana laughed. "She said she'd buy us a wedding present," she said, without mentioning the cruel way the other woman had put it.

"That doesn't sound like the Layn I know," he murmured. His eyes searched for her. "Where are you?"

"Here," she said, moving closer to him.

He caught her by the waist and drew her to him. "Did she bother you? I forget how unworldly you are. Layn can be dangerous."

"I can take care of myself," she reminded him. Her eyes studied his dark face. Was he regretting it all? Was he mourning for Layn.

"That's going to be my pleasure from now on." He suddenly lifted her clear off the ground so that her eyes were on a level with his sightless ones. "Kiss me, Dana."

Without thinking, she leaned forward and pressed her mouth very softly against his. He let her take the initiative, standing quietly while she savored the cool firmness of his lips against her own.

"You're very cool, darling," he whispered softly. "Mad at me?"

Her heart jumped at the endearment as well as the question. "No, of course not," she assured him.

"Then kiss me as if you mean it, Dana," he said, "not as if you're doing an unpleasant duty. Unless . . ." He frowned. ". . . unless it really is unpleasant?"

"Silly man," she whispered adoringly. She kissed

him again, harder this time, lingering over his firm mouth until she felt the tension drain out of him, felt the warm response of his lips, the gentle hunger of his enclosing arms.

"Better?" she teased gently, clinging to him.

"Much better," he murmured, rubbing noses. "But that's enough of that," he added with a hard sigh, setting her firmly back on her feet. "I'm no saint."

She smiled. "You're doing very well for a man who isn't."

"Yes, aren't I?" he growled. He found her hand and held it warmly as they started walking again. "Dana, you do realize that things will be . . . different . . . when we're man and wife? I won't have a marriage of convenience at my age."

"I understand," she agreed. "I don't want an artificial marriage, either. I . . . I'd like to have children." Daydreams. Wonderful daydreams. She was refusing to face facts and she knew it, but wasn't she allowed to dream just a little?

His hand contracted painfully. "Children," he whispered. "I hadn't thought of that."

"Don't you want a son?" she teased. "I thought most men did."

"Of course I do," he growled, jerking her close to his side. "It's just that I hadn't expected . . . my wife didn't want them—did Lorraine tell you? She didn't want the inconvenience."

She smiled. "Perhaps if I were beautiful and gay and worldly. . . ."

"No," he returned. "I think I know you quite

well by now. No, it wouldn't matter. You'd have your own and a dozen orphans besides, wouldn't you, and never count the cost. You'd love the whole world if it would let you."

"You make me sound saintly, and I'm not," she countered. "I'm only—"

"—a woman," he finished for her. "Yes, I know. But what a woman!" he added, bending to brush his lips over her forehead. "No regrets? Will you be sorry that I can't see our children?"

Her heart stampeded at the sound of that. *Our children.* She smiled. "No," she whispered. "I'll describe them to you in minute detail. You won't miss a thing."

His jaw tautened. He stopped, dragging her into his arms, and kissed her suddenly, hungrily, shocking her into a wild response of her own.

He released her all at once and moved away. "I'm sorry," he said curtly. "It was thinking about children. . . . We'd better go back in. I feel odd."

"Are you all right?" she asked quickly, full of concern.

"Just my head. Dana, the headaches are so much worse lately," he said pensively as they turned back toward the house. "I'm taking more and more medication, hadn't you noticed?"

She had, but she was trying not to show too much concern. "We'd better call Dr. Shane, just to play it safe, don't you think?" she asked calmly. "It's probably just the hours you've been putting in lately. More stress. It's perfectly natural."

He seemed to calm at her own easy manner. "Yes, that's probably what it is."

"But we'll have him check you over. I'll call first thing in the morning."

He nodded. "Now, no more about doctors. Let's talk about houses. Where would you like to live?"

They spent the rest of the evening talking vaguely about houses and cities and holidays and schools for the children when they came along. But Dana didn't sleep well. The headaches weren't natural, and Gannon had to know it. They were playing a game, and she was afraid of the outcome.

The next morning she called Dr. Shane and described Gannon's symptoms. He asked her to bring in her fiancé that afternoon and let him run some more tests.

She drove him to the office and sat in the waiting room while the two of them talked. Gannon reappeared, taciturn and irritable, directing her to the hospital, where he was to be admitted overnight while Dr. Shane had the tests performed. Dana was concerned about that, and she had a suspicion that something was wrong. But Dr. Shane wouldn't talk to her, and neither would Gannon, since she was now in the position of a fiancée, not a nurse.

Lorraine paced with her, worried with her. But when the test results were in and Gannon was released from the hospital, he told no one what had been found. In desperation Dana called Dr. Shane, only to be told that what he'd found was privileged information, but that she needn't worry, he was certain everything would be fine.

She approached Gannon, but he wasn't talking. He only smiled and kissed her and told her that there was a chance, just a slight one, that his sight might come back. And then she knew what was wrong with him. He was going to see again—but he didn't want to be saddled with her when it happened. He wanted Layn, and now there was a chance he could get her back. But only if Dana was out of the way.

She imparted that information to Lorraine, who laughed at her.

"You're being ridiculous, dear," she chided. "He wouldn't want Layn now, not after the way she treated him. Don't be silly. He loves you!"

But he didn't. He'd already admitted it. And now Dana was worried, terribly worried. How was she going to survive if he sent her away? She loved him so much, how was she going to let go?

Chapter Eight

Dirk came down for the next weekend, and Gannon welcomed him with unusual fervor.

"I'm glad you came," he said, thumping his brother on the back. "You can keep Dana and Lorraine company while I work on the visual aid with Al Pratt. He should be here any minute."

"Shame on you," Dirk chided. "A newly engaged man . . ."

Gannon looked briefly uncomfortable, bearing out Dana's suspicions that he hated being engaged to her, newly or not. "I know, but time is money where this new device is concerned. We've got some innovative ideas we want to work up before somebody beats us to the punch. Oh, and I've invited a guest for Sunday dinner, Lorraine," he added.

"Anyone I know, dear?" Lorraine asked without looking up from her needlepoint.

"Yes. Layn."

There was a silence in the room so utterly sudden that the sound of the woman's name seemed to echo endlessly. Dana closed her eyes, feeling her heart shatter. It was true. Now she knew it was true.

"In that case," Dirk said quietly, "I think Dana and I will drive down to Savannah for the day on Sunday."

Gannon started to speak, stopped and smiled faintly. "Perhaps that would be just as well. You might take Lorraine with you. And you might stop sounding so suspicious while you're about it," he added, the Dutch accent emphasizing itself. "It's business. Layn and I have investments together in a shipping company. We're going to discuss stock and expansion. That's all. I haven't forgotten my own engagement."

"I'm so relieved to hear it," Dirk said curtly. "If it is an engagement."

Gannon blinked. "I beg your pardon?"

"Dana isn't wearing a ring," he observed, "and I haven't heard any mention of a wedding date."

Gannon coughed. "There hasn't been time. I've been busy."

"Sure," Dirk said shortly. He jammed his hands into his pockets. "Dana, care to go for a walk with me? Pratt's just driven up, and I know Gannon will have other things on his mind."

"Of course," she said in a ghostly tone. "Lorraine, would you like to come with us Sunday? Maybe we could go back to see Katy and Maude?"

"I'd like that," Lorraine said, struggling for composure.

While they discussed times and plans, Pratt came in to join Gannon, and the two of them vanished into the study behind the closed door.

Dirk was outspoken about the Sunday dinner and angrier than Dana had seen him since they became acquainted.

"Layn here," he growled. "And when he's engaged to you! He might consider your feelings. Lorraine told me what she said to you in town!"

"He doesn't know what she said," she told him quietly. "I didn't think it was necessary to tell him. I can handle Layn myself."

"So you think," he returned darkly. "She'd cut you into ribbons, and you know it. She's been after Gannon for a long time, despite the fact that she ran after the accident. I've always thought it was as much because she thought he'd blame her as because she didn't want to be around a blind man."

"Did he love her very much?" she asked.

"I don't know my brother that well. He's very good at disguising his feelings." He shrugged. "But they were together most of the time until he was blinded."

She felt sick all over. And now it was starting again: She was going to lose him. And there was nothing she could do. She didn't have the weapons to fight a woman like Layn.

"Maybe it really is business," she said softly.

"Maybe cows will run computers," he scoffed. "Don't kid yourself, honey; they don't need to meet here on a Sunday to do something they could manage over the phone."

Tears sprung to her eyes, but she blinked them away, too proud to let him see how hurt she was.

"I'm sorry," he said quietly. "I shouldn't have said that. It could be innocent. . . ."

"You don't have to tell me something I already know," she said softly. "He doesn't love me; he said as much."

"But you love him very much."

She nodded. "Fortunes of war," she laughed bitterly. "The first time in my life, and it had to be a man like Gannon. . . . If only I were beautiful and worldly and sophisticated!"

"You wouldn't be the girl you are," he corrected. "I like you as you are. So does he."

"Like," she agreed. "Not love. And it wouldn't be enough, eventually. It's just as well. I'll be sad for a while, but I'll get over him."

"Will you really?" he asked, eyeing her.

She turned away. "Let's go look for sand crabs. They fascinate me, the way they dive into the sand to hide. Look, there's one . . . !"

He watched her with sad eyes, wishing there was something he could do to ease the pain she was trying to hide. But he was as helpless s she was.

Dana had been hoping that the other woman wouldn't show up until after she and Dirk and

Lorraine had left the house on Sunday. But as luck would have it, Layn was on the doorstep before Lorraine had finished dressing.

"Well, hello, darling," she told Dirk as he answered the door. She was resplendent in a sea-blue dress with white accessories and a matching scarf tied over her hair, looking the fashion plate she was.

Layn's eyes darted past him to Dana, and she gave the other girl's simple white sun dress and sandals a distastefully quick appraisal.

"I'm not too early?" Layn murmured.

"Of course not, darling," Dirk replied with sweet sarcasm. "Gannon's waiting for you in his study. The rest of us are off to Savannah for the day."

Layn looked faintly shocked. "Leaving poor Gannon all alone with me?"

"We could load a gun for him before we leave," Dirk suggested.

Layn only laughed. "You might load one for me," she murmured, glancing at Dana. "Since he's been keeping company with the little saint, he may be desperate for some wicked company."

Dana's eyebrows lifted. "Think so? I'll have to remember to polish my halo more often."

Layn became angry when she couldn't get a rise out of Dana, then whirled on her heel and stalked off into the study.

Dirk was trying to smother his laughter and failing miserably. "You wicked lady!" he burst out.

Dana only shrugged. "Well, she asked for it. Shall we wait for Lorraine in the car?"

But just about that time Lorraine came quickly down the stairs to join them, and they left without even a good-bye to Gannon.

It was a long day. Dana, despite the fact that she enjoyed visiting Katy and Maude, spent most of the hours brooding on what was going on back at the house. Was Layn right? Would he be so desperate for a woman that he'd make a dead set at her? Was he tired of Dana's repressive ways? Was he trying to find a way out of the engagement? Why else would he have flaunted Layn in front of her?

They stopped at a restaurant for lunch, and while Lorraine was creating a salad at the salad bar, Dirk leaned forward earnestly.

"Worried?" he asked softly. "You've hardly smiled all day."

Dana smiled faintly. "Yes, I'm worried. How can I compete with somebody who looks like Miss Dalmont?"

"Easily, since Gannon can't see her," he replied brutally.

"That's not what I meant. He's seen her; he's never seen me." She toyed with her napkin. "Besides that, he's not a saint. I must be a drag to him. . . ."

"He adores you. It's even obvious to someone as thick-skinned as myself." He reached over and touched her hand. "Come on, spill it."

She lifted her shoulders. "I think he's trying to make me leave."

He frowned. "Why?"

"It's not something I can explain. But ever since he went back to the doctor, he's been distant with me. I can't get close to him." She looked up, worry shadowing her eyes. "They told him his sight was very likely to return—something about the shrapnel that they wouldn't tell me. What if he's beginning to see again?" she groaned. "Compared to Layn, I'm so ugly—and he loved her! Now she's back and he's asked her to dinner. . . ."

He caught her hand in his and held it gently. "You're not ugly. You're a lovely woman, and any man would be proud to marry you. Even me, the confirmed bachelor, if I thought I had a chance."

She blinked, not believing him.

"Think I'm kidding?" he mused. "I'm not. There's a quality in you that I've never seen in another woman, and I like it very much. If Gannon didn't have a place in your heart, I'd give him a run for his money."

She blushed softly and lowered her eyes on a smile. "Thank you. You don't know what you've done for my crushed ego."

"I wasn't flattering you."

"Yes, I know." She lifted her eyes again. "He wants Layn, you know."

He sighed wearily. "Yes."

"I won't hold him to a promise he made in a moment of weakness. The minute his sight is restored, I'm going home to Ashton," she said firmly.

"You might consider fighting for him," he reminded her.

"With what?" She laughed. "I don't have potent weapons, and even if I did, I wouldn't use them. I'm not the type. No, he'd have to love me. And he's already admitted that he doesn't. It would be a very empty kind of relationship—don't you think?—if all the love was on one side."

He nodded solemnly. "I suppose so. Dana, if you do go home, I'd like to see you again."

She smiled. "I'd like that too."

He grinned. "Now we're getting somewhere. Tell me about your work."

They started discussing the advances in medicine when Lorraine joined them, and then the talk switched to flowers and gardens for the rest of the meal.

Gannon was alone when they returned to the house; he was preoccupied. He let Dana bring his meal and they sat in a cool silence for a long time while he finished it and asked her to pour him a second cup of coffee.

"Did you have a nice day?" he asked absently.

"Oh, it was lovely. Katy and Maude send their love."

He laughed bitterly. "Just what I need."

She paled, turning her attention to the coffee cup. "Did you get your business straightened out?"

He leaned back in the chair with the cup in his hands. "Yes. Layn's very lovely, isn't she?"

"Very," she agreed.

"Poised, sophisticated . . . with an excellent business head. The kind of wife a businessman could depend on to help him accomplish his goals," he added; his point seemed to have been made deliberately. He sipped his coffee. "What was she wearing?"

"Blue," she said, staring into her own cup. "Sea blue."

He chuckled. "One of her favorite colors. I remember a bathing suit she used to have, when I took her to Nassau. . . ." His face clouded and he stopped abruptly, swinging forward in the chair. "How are you at taking dictation?" he asked suddenly. "I need to write some letters, and I'm not fast enough with the computer yet. Can you type?"

"Yes to both," she said agreeably. "I'll be glad to help you."

"Yes, I know," he said under his breath, and looked as if he were hurting inside. He leaned back wearily in his chair and closed his eyes. "It doesn't help the situation."

She moved closer to the desk, studying his lined face. "Gannon, is your sight returning?"

He made a curt movement, his sightless eyes opening on darkness. "What?"

"Are you beginning to see again?" she persisted. "I know something's happened—I can feel it. You're . . . you're very distant lately."

He laughed harshly. "Am I? And why do you suppose I am?"

She studied her feet. "Layn's very beautiful," she said quietly.

He sat breathing steadily, deliberately. "Yes."

"And you . . . you cared for her before you were blinded."

"That too." He cocked his head, listening. When she didn't say anything more, he seemed to slump. "She blamed herself, you know," he said finally. "She was driving the speedboat. It's taken her all this time to come to grips with it and realize that I didn't blame her."

Dana didn't believe that for a minute, but she kept quiet. More than likely, the knowledge that Gannon's sight was returning had a great deal to do with Layn's sudden interest in him.

"We're very different, aren't we?" she asked softly. "You and I, I mean. From different backgrounds, different worlds."

He was listening intently, his face shuttered. "Yes, we are," he said. "And I hate to say it, Dana, but when I . . . regain my sight, that difference is going to become even more apparent. I travel in circles you've never touched, full of wild living and unconventional people."

She watched him with a heart that felt near breaking. "And, too, there's Layn, isn't there?" she prodded. "Layn, who would fit very well—does fit very well—in that kind of world?"

His face tautened. "Yes."

She lifted her hands to her waist and clasped them there, very tightly. "Gannon, about the engagement . . ."

"Not today," he said curtly, as if the words were being dragged out of him, as if he hadn't meant to say them. "We'll discuss it some other time. Get that pad, please. Layn's driving me down to Savannah the day after tomorrow for a meeting about that expansion I mentioned at the shipyard. I'll be gone most of the day, and I need to have this correspondence out of the way before we get there."

"Yes," she said quickly.

She turned and almost ran from the room, feeling as if something inside her had died. He wanted out. If she'd been blind herself, she'd have sensed it today, when he spoke so lovingly of Layn and seemed to hate the very thought of regaining his sight because he was tied to a woman he only needed because he was blind. And when he could see, he'd only want Layn. . . .

By the morning Gannon was about to go off with Layn, Dana was more than ready to have the luxury of a day without his company. He was taciturn and curt and he began to pick at her as he had in the early days of their acquaintance. The engagement, while still apparently in force, was never referred to, and he treated her as his nurse, not his wife-to-be.

"I asked you to get Al Pratt on the phone half an hour ago," he snarled at her just before Layn arrived. "Have you even tried?"

"Yes, I have," she said coldly. "He wasn't in. I am not a miracle worker; I can't produce people at a second's notice."

"You might be a little more diligent," he accused.

"I took my training in medicine, not business," she reminded him coldly.

"You have a sharp tongue," he growled.

"Yours is sharper, and you have no patience anymore," she shot back. She felt herself begin to slump. "It's a good thing you're going out," she said wearily. "Perhaps being with Miss Dalmont will improve your temper."

His nostrils flared. "Perhaps it will. At least she tries to please me once in a while, miss."

So might I, if I knew what you wanted of me, she thought miserably. She moved away from him, her nurse's uniform making clean, crisp sounds in the silent room. She'd started wearing it again, because it made her feel more comfortable. He was treating her like his nurse, not his fiancée, after all, so what did it matter?

His head rose suddenly. "What's that noise?" he asked sharply.

"Sir?"

"That rustling sound. . . ."

"My uniform," she said coldly.

He actually seemed to blanche. "I thought you were wearing street clothes now."

"I came here as, and still am, your nurse," she reminded him with dignity. "Is it surprising that I feel more secure dressed to fit the part?"

He stood quietly, breathing deliberately. "We're engaged," he said.

She laughed softly, bitterly. "No, sir," she told

him. "That was a bit of fiction. An impulsive, quickly regretted and impossibly answered proposal that would be best forgotten by both of us."

"You don't want to marry me?" he asked, something odd in his tone.

"No, sir, I don't," she lied, her voice carrying a conviction that was not in her heart. "As we've already agreed, our worlds are too different ever to mix. And when you have your sight again, the last thing you'll want or need is a scarred, plain little . . ."

"Stop it!" he burst out, white in the face.

She caught her breath at the violence in the harsh words, at the expression in his blank eyes. But before she could say a word or question him, there was a loud knock at the door, and she went quietly to answer it.

Layn gave her a lazy, cool appraisal. "Back in chains, I see," she said pleasantly, chic in a white linen suit with a pale pink silk blouse. "Where's Gannon?"

"In his study, of course. He's expecting you," Dana said quietly.

"Do show me in," came the amused reply.

As if she needed showing. But Dana complied. There was no fight left in her.

"Miss Dalmont is here," Dana said to Gannon's rigid back.

He turned, staring toward the sound of her voice. "Layn?"

"Right here, darling," she cooed, going to him.

She reached up and kissed him, and to Dana's amazement his arms went around her and he returned the kiss with a hungry fervor that was faintly embarrassing.

"What a nice greeting," Layn gasped when he let go. "Just like old times!"

"You smell delicious—just like old times," he murmured. "Ready to go?"

"Whenever you are."

Gannon took Layn's slender hand while Dana stood and watched them, hurting all the way to the heels of her comfortable shoes.

"You aren't taking your little nurse, I hope?" Layn asked.

Gannon flushed darkly and seemed about to say something, but stifled it. "No, Dana isn't coming with us," he said instead.

"Thank goodness," Layn murmured fervently. "Come, Gannon, the car's just outside. I hope we won't need an umbrella, because I didn't bring one. It's getting very dark and stormy-looking out."

"Dana?" Gannon hesitated.

She swallowed, full of hurt pride and rejection. "Yes?"

He seemed to flinch. "Don't go out on the beach alone, will you? There are storm warnings out today."

"I won't," she promised quietly.

"I wish I could believe you," he said under his breath.

She didn't bother to reply, standing aside as he went out the door with Layn. Dana closed it behind them, just before she burst into tears.

"You're very quiet this afternoon," Lorraine remarked just before dinner that night as they sat together in the living room while thunder and lightning raged outside. "Does the storm bother you?"

Dana shook her head. "Not at all."

"Gannon's going out with Layn does, though, doesn't it?" the older woman probed gently. "Oh, Dana, if I only understood my stepson . . ."

"It's all very simple," Dana told her. She looked up with sad, quiet eyes. "He wants me to break off the engagement. He's done everything but toss me out the window to get his point across."

"But why?"

"His sight is coming back," she said, sure of it now. "He told me quite bluntly that I wouldn't fit into his world—the world he lives in when he has his sight. I could only belong in a world we made together, out of darkness. Layn is back and he wants her. And who could blame him?" she added bitterly. "She's perfect, so sophisticated and worldly . . ."

"So selfish and shallow," Lorraine countered angrily. "Your exact opposite in every way. It isn't like Gannon to succumb to that woman after the way she's treated him. He's much too proud. And he cares for you. It's in the way he speaks to you, the way he listens for your step and the way his face lights up when you walk into a room. No, there's something else, I'm sure of it."

But Dana wasn't convinced. Gannon's hunger for Layn had been all too obvious in the kiss she'd seen them share, and his manner with Dana had convinced her that all he wanted now was to be rid of her.

"When he comes back tonight," Dana said quietly, "I'm going to break off the engagement. It's what he wants, and now it's what I want too. If I'm right, he'll get back on his feet that much faster because he has Layn to look forward to."

"Dana, I wish you'd wait—just a little longer," Lorraine said softly.

"There's no point. If he felt as I did, it would be different. But I have no right to build my happiness on his sorrow. I won't."

"You must love him very much, my dear, to care so much about his happiness."

Dana's eyes clouded. "I'll never love anyone else. Not as long as I live. But I can't marry him, knowing how he really feels."

Lorraine looked as if she wanted badly to say something else, but she smiled sadly and went back to her needlepoint. There was no use.

Chapter Nine

It didn't help Dana's already damaged pride when Gannon called an hour later to tell Lorraine that he and Layn were going to spend the night in Savannah.

"He said Layn's afraid to drive back with the weather so bad," Lorraine related irritably. "If you want my opinion, she just wants Gannon all to herself."

"That's very likely," Dana said wearily. "Can you blame her?"

"For more than you know, I can blame her," the older woman said curtly. "Dirk's coming in the morning. Perhaps he can make some sense of all this. Heaven knows, I can't!"

But Dana could. Not that it eased the hurt. It made it worse.

The night was horrible. The thunder and lightning seemed to go on forever, and Dana couldn't sleep for its crash and roar. The ocean was boiling with the force of the storm, like the one raging inside Dana.

It seemed such a long time since she'd come there from Ashton, full of guilt and grief and despair. And while she was still aching from Gannon's rejection, she felt that she'd begun to cope very well with her personal problems. The sharp edge of grief was beginning to numb.

She went to stand at the window and watched the lightning flash down toward the water. Death was, after all, as natural as the lightning, as the rain. It was the routine progression of things—birth, life, and death; a cycle that everything human had to follow. And somewhere in that natural progression was God's master plan. Even Mandy had had a part in that, and so did her death and the manner of it. It wasn't for Dana to question why. It was her part to do as God directed.

She wrapped her arms tightly around her thin nightgown with a ragged sigh. Perhaps her presence here had helped Gannon in some small way to rethink his own life. Even if she lost him forever, she felt that she'd helped him see a sense of purpose and meaning in his existence. And wasn't that worth a few tears? After all, love in its ideal form was an unselfish thing. If she loved him, she had to want what was best for him, didn't she?

A silent word to God, seeking His guidance, brought comfort. Resolutely she dried her eyes and went back to bed, and slept peacefully for the first time in days.

Dirk came in the door just as Lorraine and Dana were sitting down to breakfast, and slid into a chair between them to dig hungrily into bacon and eggs and homemade biscuits.

"I didn't realize how hungry I was," he chuckled, watching their amused glances. "Where's Gannon? Sleeping late?"

"He's in Savannah," Lorraine said tautly. "He and Layn didn't drive back last night. She said she was afraid of the weather."

"That's a laugh," Dirk scoffed. "Kidnapped him, did she?"

"Looks like it," the older woman replied. She glanced at Dana. "I don't know what's wrong with him lately; he acts so . . . strange."

Dana put down her napkin. "Excuse me," she said. "I'm through, and I do love to walk along the beach early in the morning. The rain's gone, and it's so lovely . . ." she realized that she was rambling, but she tacked on a quick smile and rushed out before anyone could stop her.

She'd only gotten halfway down to the pier before Dirk caught up with her.

"Hold up and I'll stroll along with you," he said. "How are things with you and Gannon?"

"Things aren't," she said shortly. "I broke the engagement."

"You what?"

"I had to," she burst out. "He was hating every second of it. Layn came, and the way he kissed her . . . Oh, Dirk, he loves her, don't you know?"

She burst into tears, and he drew her gently into his arms, holding her quietly while she got some of the hurt and pain out of her system.

"I'm sorry," she muttered. "I can't seem to stop crying lately."

"He really is blind if he can't feel how much you love him," he growled.

"He knows I love him. He can't help wanting Layn, can he?" she murmured quietly. She drew away and dabbed at her eyes. "I wish I could go home. Facing my kinfolk now isn't nearly as anguishing as having to live around Gannon day after day and knowing he wishes I were in some other country."

"Poor Dana," he said softly. "I wish there was something I could do to help."

She drew in a steadying breath. "But there isn't. I'll just have to wait it out. I can't leave him, not yet, not until he sends me away."

"As long as he needs you, is that how this goes?"

She nodded. "As long as he needs me." She smiled wanly. "I only hope it won't be much longer. I don't know if I can bear much more."

"That makes two of us," he muttered.

But she had her eyes on the horizon, and her mind was with Gannon. Where was he? Why didn't he come home?

The day passed slowly, and Dana's troubled eyes

kept going to the driveway. But no car came. By the time the cook was putting supper on the table, Gannon still hadn't appeared.

When the phone rang, Dana rushed to answer it. Lorraine was still upstairs and Dirk had gone, and there was no one else around.

"Hello?" she said quickly.

"Dana?"

It was Gannon's deep voice, and her knees felt rubbery. She sat down in the chair beside the table. "Yes. Gannon, are you all right?"

There was a pregnant pause. "Yes," he said, his voice sounding strained and terse. "As a matter of fact, I have some rather exciting news, Dana. I've got my sight back."

"What!" she exclaimed, sitting up straight.

"We were rushing to get back to the hotel in the rain," he said quietly, "and I tripped and fell. The blow must have dislodged the shrapnel, because I can see."

Tears were rolling down her cheeks unashamedly. "Oh, Gannon, I'm so happy for you. So happy!"

There was another long pause, and a long, shuddering sigh. "Yes. Well, you do understand what that means?"

All the joy washed away in a torrent of cold understanding. Yes, she understood. She was out of a job. Sighted, he didn't need her anymore.

She swallowed down another burst of tears. "I understand," she said on a whisper. "You . . . you won't need a nurse now, will you?" she laughed.

"No," he said tersely. "Dana . . . about our engagement?"

"What engagement?" she asked bravely. "It's all right, you don't have to pull your punches. We agreed already that it was a mistake, that . . . that I wouldn't fit into your world, didn't we? Anyway, Dirk was here . . ."

His voice was colder than she'd ever heard it before. "Dirk? Well, well, how very convenient. Trying to get his bid in, is he?"

"That's unfair," she returned. "Especially when you as much as told me that you didn't want me anymore!"

There was a long, hot silence on the other end of the line. "Yes, I said that, didn't I?" he asked, his voice odd and deep.

"It's just as well. I . . . I miss my home," she said after a minute, her lower lip trembling. She controlled it with an effort. "It's time I went back, made my peace with my people."

"When did you plan to go?" he asked curtly.

She cleared her throat. "I . . . I thought . . . in the morning."

He sounded relieved. "That would be a good time. I . . . I plan to stay here with Layn for a few more days."

Her eyes closed on a pain so sweeping that she thought she might fall to her knees. "Then it will work out . . . very well for you, won't it? She's so lovely."

There was a harsh, muffled sound. "It isn't because of the way you look!" he burst out. "Sweet heaven, Dana, I'd give anything to make you understand!"

"There's nothing to understand, and you don't owe me any explanations," she said quietly, gripping the phone like a lifeline. "I came here as your nurse. You were lonely and maybe a little afraid. . . . Didn't I tell you that most male patients make a grab for their nurses? I didn't take you seriously, of course."

They both knew it was a lie, but he was going along with the fiction to help save her pride. She hated knowing that.

"I'm glad of that," he said roughly. There was another pause, a longer one. "If I can do anything for you, ever . . ."

"I can take care of myself," she told him proudly. "But thank you for offering. Shall I tell Lorraine and Dirk . . . ?"

"No!" he said quickly. "No," he added in a more controlled tone. "I want to surprise them when I get back. Promise me you won't say a word."

"As you like," she agreed dully. "But why shall I say I'm going home?"

"Can't you invent an emergency?" he asked. "Or is telling a white lie too much for your snowy conscience?"

She swallowed down a hot retort. "I can manage that, I think."

"Good. Then do so. For all they have to know, this phone call could have been from your people. You don't have to say it was me, do you?"

"No," she agreed. "There's no one around right

now. I'll . . . I'll find an excuse to take the first bus out in the morning. Gannon . . . I'm very happy for you."

He didn't reply right away. "I hope things go well for you," he said finally, heavily. "Be happy, Dana. I'd give anything if . . ."

"If," she murmured. "What a sad word."

"Sadder than you know, little one," he whispered. "Good-bye, my . . . Dana."

"Good-bye, Gannon."

The line went dead. She put her head in her hands and cried until there were no tears left. It was over, all over. He didn't want her anymore, and he couldn't possibly have made it any plainer. He wanted Layn. Beautiful, poised Layn, who was sophisticated and physically perfect.

Dana heard Lorraine coming down the staircase minutes later, and was grateful that she'd had a little time to compose herself. She drew herself erect and tried to look calm.

"Did I hear the phone ring, dear?" Lorraine asked with a smile.

"Yes," Dana said, thinking fast. "It was my aunt. She's developed a serious medical problem, and there's no one but me to look after her. I don't know what to do . . ." She let her voice trail off and couldn't look at the older woman.

"Do? Why, you must go and see about her," Lorraine said quickly. "I can manage Gannon, with Dirk's help. We can do without you if we must," she added gently.

Dana felt dreadful. She'd hated telling the lie,

but it was the only way she could think of to do as Gannon had asked. Besides, she thought miserably, when he came back home and Lorraine realized that he could see again, it would all come right anyway. And Aunt Helen did have a serious medical problem, after all—her sharp and unthinking tongue.

"I'd better pack, then. You'll . . . explain to Mr. van der Vere when he comes home?" she asked, pausing on the lowest step of the staircase.

"I can't tell you how sorry I am that things didn't work out for the two of you," came the soft reply. "Layn will never make him happy, Dana. She's too shallow to give anything of herself. But men are so strange, my dear."

Dana smiled wistfully. "I have to agree that they seem it sometimes. I hope you'll keep in touch with me; I'd like to know how Mr. van der Vere does."

Lorraine frowned slightly. "But surely you'll be coming back?"

Dana cleared her throat. "Oh, I'm planning to, of course," she lied calmly. "But one never knows how things will turn out. It could be days or even weeks before I can leave Aunt Helen. And she is my only remaining relative—except for my father."

"I've grown very fond of you, Dana." Lorraine hugged her gently and kissed her pale cheek. "Don't worry about Gannon, will you? I'll take care of him. And there's every chance that he'll see through Layn's wiles eventually. Isn't there a saying that all things come to he who waits?"

"If he who waits lives long enough, I suppose,"

Dana said with an attempt at humor. She drew away with a sigh. "Do let me hear how things go."

Lorraine nodded. "I certainly will. Give my love to Mrs. Pibbs, will you?"

Dana smiled, remembering her supervisor. With any luck at all, she just might be able to get another job at the hospital. Of course, she'd have to swear Mrs. Pibbs to secrecy, so that she wouldn't let anything slip about Aunt Helen being in the bloom of good health. . . .

"I will. I suppose I'd better get packed. I'll want to catch the first bus out in the morning."

"Gannon may be home tonight," Lorraine mentioned.

Dana almost assured her that he wouldn't be, but she bit her tongue. "Yes, he may," she said instead, and managed a wan smile.

"Don't you want to eat first?" the older woman asked.

Dana hesitated. But her stomach did feel empty, and starving herself wasn't going to help the situation. "Yes, I think I will," she said. She followed Lorraine into the dining room. But she didn't taste anything she ate.

Chapter Ten

Ashton hadn't changed in the weeks Dana had been away: It was still slow-moving and provincial and charming. But she thought when she got to the bus depot that she was going to miss the sound of the ocean at night, miss the whitecaps on the beach. Most of all she was going to miss Gannon, and that was going to be the hardest adjustment to make.

She got off the bus, suitcase in hand, and called Jenny. Luckily she was at the apartment and not working.

"You're back!" her friend exclaimed. "Am I glad! My other roommate got sick of picking up after me and moved out, and I'm so lonely—and there's a job available if you hurry! Mrs. Pibbs would give it to you; I know she would!"

Dana smiled gaily. Everything was working out fine; the path was being smoothed ahead of her. For the first time in two days she felt a ray of hope for her life.

Mrs. Pibbs was waiting for her in the spotless office, looking puzzled but pleased.

"All right, Nurse, let's start at the beginning, if you please," she said curtly, leaning back in her chair to listen.

It was useless to put on a front with Mrs. Pibbs, who had a mind like a net. With a sigh Dana told her the whole wretched story, leaving out nothing.

"So I made up the fiction of Aunt Helen needing me and came home," she said quietly, avoiding the other woman's probing eyes.

"Are you certain that he was telling you the truth?" the supervisor asked shrewdly.

"Why should he lie?" Dana asked reasonably. "At any rate he wanted to be rid of me and the fiction of our engagement, and now he is. And there's Miss Dalmont. . . ."

Whatever Mrs. Pibbs was thinking, she obviously decided to keep to herself. She leaned forward. "Very well, when I speak with Lorraine, I won't blow your cover. But in fact your Aunt Helen could use some support right now. She's grieving over what she said to you before you left Ashton. I think she'd be grateful for the opportunity to see you and apologize."

Dana smiled. "I'd like to see her too. I've had a lot of time to think since I've been away. I think I've come to grips with it all now."

Mrs. Pibbs lifted her eyebrows. "God's will?"

The younger woman nodded. "God's will. I won't question it anymore."

"Just as well too. Now, here's the job that's open. It's only night supervisor on the east wing, but you'll make a go of it, I'm sure. You have only to readjust to the new schedule, or have you been keeping late nights anyway?"

"Mr. van der Vere liked to talk into the early hours," Dana confessed. "I've been staying up relatively late, so it shouldn't be too difficult to get used to the eleven-to-seven shift again."

"Good girl. And Jenny tells me she's without a roommate," she added, glancing at Dana's suitcase on the floor beside her chair.

"Yes, ma'am," Dana laughed. She got to her feet. "With your permission I'll dash over and stow my luggage. Do I start tonight?"

"With my blessing." Mrs. Pibbs actually smiled. "Welcome home, Dana."

"Thank you," she replied earnestly.

Dana unpacked, having barely enough time to say hello and good-bye to Jenny, who went on duty minutes later. Then, when she'd rested for a few minutes, she resolutely lifted the receiver of the phone and dialed Aunt Helen's number.

It rang five times before it was picked up, and Dana had almost given up when she heard her aunt's honeyed tones on the other end of the line.

"Aunt Helen?" she asked hesitantly.

"Dana! Dana, is it you? Oh, my dear, I've been

sick to death about what I said to you. . . . Can you ever forgive me?"

"Of course I can, you were hurting just as much as I was," Dana said on a sigh. It was such a blessed relief to have things patched up again. "How are you?"

"Can you come over?" Aunt Helen asked, ignoring the question. "I'll make a pot of coffee and we'll talk, all right?"

"I'll be there in ten minutes," she replied.

It took fifteen, by the time she changed into jeans and a T-shirt, but her aunt lived only about two blocks from the apartment.

Helen's house was an old, rambling white frame Victorian, with a long front porch where white rocking chairs and an equally white porch swing invited visitors to sit among the potted flowers that lined the entire porch. Helen came rushing out, still wearing her apron, and grabbed Dana in a crushing embrace. She was crying, and Dana cried too.

Helen dabbed at her eyes through a smile and handed Dana a tissue.

"Silly women," she muttered. "Want to have our coffee out here?"

"I'd love it," Dana replied. "Can I help?"

"No, the tray's all fixed. My best silver, too, I want you to know."

"I'm honored!"

Helen disappeared into the house and returned with a huge silver tray laden with cake and cookies and coffee.

She put it on the white wrought-iron table by the rocking chairs and invited Dana to sit down. It was delightful on the porch, cool and quiet and homey. Dana could remember so many lazy summer days spent there while Mandy visited her only sister.

"How are you?" Helen asked while they sipped coffee and nibbled on homemade cookies.

"I'm better. Much better. And you?"

Helen shrugged. "Getting over it, I suppose. I still miss her, as I'm sure you do. But life goes on, doesn't it?"

Dana smiled wistfully. "Inevitably." She finished a cookie and took a sip of black coffee. "How's Dad?"

Helen gave her a sharp, probing look. "Hurting. He thinks you blame him for Mandy's death. He calls me once a week to see how you're doing."

That was painful. "It was hard," she said after a minute, "getting used to being two families, when we'd been one most of my life. Always it was Mom and Dad. Now it's Dad and someone else, and no Mom." She sighed bitterly. "I honestly feel like an orphan."

"Dear, we've agreed that life goes on. Now answer me just one question honestly," Helen said, leaning forward intently. "Would you want your father to live all his life alone, with no one?"

Dana blinked. "Well, no, I don't suppose so."

"Would you want him to be a playboy and take out a different woman every night?"

"No!" Dana said, horrified.

"You've never even met Sharla formally," Dana

was reminded. "She's a lovely woman, Dana. Very old-fashioned and sweet. She likes to cook and grow flowers and do needlepoint, and she loves the whole world. She's a . . . motherly woman. And she has no children of her own; she'd never been married before she met Jack."

That was interesting. Dana sat up straight, staring across at her aunt. "She hadn't?"

Helen smiled. "No, she hadn't. So, you see, marriage was a very special thing for her. She can't have children anymore, of course, and she was looking forward to having a grown daughter."

Tears stung Dana's eyes. She turned away. "That might be nice, to be wanted by someone," she whispered.

Helen frowned. "Whatever do you mean, darling?"

"Mother told me."

Helen blinked. "Told you what?"

"That because of me, Dad and Mom had to get married. That he never wanted me, that he blamed me for being the cause of a marriage they both hated," she said, letting the bitterness and hurt pour out.

Helen got up and drew the weeping girl into her arms. "How could Mandy tell you such a thing?" she ground out, rocking Dana slowly. "It wasn't true! They'd been married over a year when you came along. And your father was the one who wanted you, my dear, as much as I hate to admit it. Mandy wasn't domestic, even in those early years. She hated the restriction of a child and refused to have another one. You spent so much of those early years with me, didn't you know?" she added wistfully, tears welling in her eyes. "Mandy would leave you with me while she partied. And since I had no children and no husband, you became the light of my life. You still are."

Dana wept unashamedly. "Why did she tell me that—why?"

"Because she'd grown bitter with advancing age, darling," Helen said soothingly. "She was unhappy and afraid of being alone, and she wanted to make you hate Jack for her own misery. He did try, Dana, he did. But your mother was such an unhappy person. Eventually she turned to alcohol because she couldn't endure reality. Her whole life turned into a waking nightmare. She would have destroyed the entire family if she'd lived, and you know it. Don't you, Dana?"

Dana's lower lip trembled. "Yes," she ground out. "I knew it all along, but it hurt so much to admit it. And I felt guilty. . . ."

"That was my fault. I always say the wrong thing, and I never blamed you; I was just hysterical." She drew back. "Dana, it was God's will. He decides the hour of death, not you and I. And Mandy's so much happier now with Him, don't you imagine?"

Dana smiled wetly. "Yes, I imagine she is. I just miss her so!"

"I miss her too. But we want what's best for her, after all. And she's at peace."

Dana nodded, dabbing again at the tears. "How about some more coffee?" she asked.

"Suits me. Some more cookies too?"

"I'd like that." She sat back and accepted a second cup of steaming black coffee. "Aunt Helen, would you tell me some more about Sharla?" she asked after a minute.

Helen turned away to pour her own coffee, smiling secretly before she sat back and began to talk.

By the end of the second week Dana was back in the swing of things. The only hard moment had come when, catching a late-night newscast with Jenny, she'd seen Gannon van der Vere being interviewed by one of the anchormen.

"Say, isn't that the man you worked for? What a dish!" Jenny exclaimed, leaning forward to watch the screen intently.

Dana felt her face go white as she looked again into those deep-set eyes as Gannon's tanned face filled the screen. Her heart did a backflip just from her looking at him, looking into the eyes that could quite plainly see again.

"My own struggle with blindness," Gannon was saying, "taught me the value of proper tools to cope with it. This new device we're working on is a revolutionary concept. It will translate forms and shapes into a kind of braille that can be read by the holder's fingers, giving him the pattern of places and even people and traffic directly ahead of him. The impulses will be fed onto a screen in a piece of equipment about the size of a portable cassette player. In theory it's quite unique. We hope that theory will translate well into a useful product."

"Amazing," the newsman murmured. "Mr. van der Vere, we've heard that your company may take a tremendous loss on this particular product to make it affordable to the general public."

"That is so," Gannon replied quietly. "In order to be effective, it must be accessible to the people who need it. We're cutting corners to keep the cost of production down, and in cases of dire need we plan to have a loan program as well."

"Would you term that good business?" the newsman asked dryly.

"A question of definitions," Gannon replied. "Our stockholders have no complaints about their profit, and one such sideline as this shouldn't have any disastrous effect on our finances. However, before I'll let the stockholders lose one penny, I'll pay for this new product out of my own pocket. I've been there, you see," he added softly. "I know what it is to be blind. I think those of us who are sighted and have access to the technology are morally obliged to help those less fortunate."

"Philanthropy, Mr. van der Vere?"

He laughed softly. "God's business, sir," he replied with a grin.

The interviewer asked several more questions, but Dana didn't hear them. She was lost in the pleasure of what she'd already heard.

"Isn't he a dish?" Jenny said in awe when the interview was over and the screen was blank. "How in the world were you able to drag yourself away from him?"

"Oh, I managed," Dana hedged. She'd told

Jenny nothing about what had really happened during her absence. And she wasn't going to. It was too painful to rehash.

Friday night came and she dressed very carefully for dinner with Aunt Helen. She chose an off-white shirtwaist dress with red accessories and a flashy red scarf, letting her long pale hair stay loose and free. She didn't know why her aunt had insisted on such formality, but then, Helen did occasionally get eccentric.

Of course, there was another possibility too—one Dana was afraid to ponder. She'd mentioned to Helen that she wanted very much to meet Sharla and make her peace with her father, but was too ashamed of her own behavior to approach him and risk another rejection. Helen had murmured something about things working out and had gone about her business. But this dinner sounded faintly suspicious.

Sure enough, when Dana got to Helen's house, there was a strange car parked in the driveway. She gripped her purse as if it threatened to escape, and forced herself to walk onto the porch and ring the doorbell.

Helen came rushing to answer it, her face flushed, her eyes apprehensive.

"There you are," she said, opening the door. "Come in, come in. Uh, I invited two more for supper. . . ."

As Dana entered the living room, she came face-to-face with her father and Sharla, and she felt all the blood drain slowly out of her cheeks.

Chapter Eleven

"Dana, I'd like you to meet Sharla," Helen said, faintly ruffled as she dragged Dana forward. "I think it's about time the two of you were formally introduced."

Sharla was tall and slender, with whitish-gold hair and pale blue eyes. She looked as nervous as Dana felt, but she looked delightful in a simple cotton shirtwaist that mirrored Dana's own unruffled style of dressing.

"Hello," Sharla said, extending a hand. She smiled hesitantly. "I . . . I wanted to meet you before, but . . ."

Dana nodded, taking the hand. It was warm and strong, and it was a hand that was no stranger to housework—a far cry from Mandy's delicate, well-manicured ones.

"How are you?" Jack Steele asked quietly, watching his daughter closely. "Helen said you'd completely recovered, and you . . . look well."

"I'm doing nicely, thanks," Dana replied. Her eyes scanned the familiar face, finding new lines and new gray hairs. He looked older, tired. But there was a light in his eyes when he glanced down at Sharla that she'd never seen before. The same light she knew was in her own when she'd looked at Gannon.

She glanced away, embarrassed.

"Sharla, why don't you help me with supper?" Helen said, with a meaningful glance toward father and daughter.

Sharla joined her quickly. "I'd love to."

When the other women were gone, Dana shifted from one foot to the other uncomfortably, searching for words.

"I've been worried," Jack Steele said finally, hesitantly. He shrugged. "I wanted to call you, but we've been so far apart for so long, and I knew I wasn't on your list of favorite people. I just let the time go by, I guess."

She nodded. She clasped her hands in front of her. "Yes, I know. That's how it was for me too."

"I didn't marry Mandy because I had to," he blurted out, avoiding her eyes. "I loved her. I really loved her, Dana. But when you came along, and she refused to settle down and take care of you—when she began enjoying parties and alcohol more than she enjoyed her marriage and her daughter—" He lifted his hands helplessly. "I don't even remember when it stopped being love. One day I woke up and realized that my life was too empty to bear. I thought if we divorced, perhaps she could find love again in someone or something. I didn't expect that she'd deteriorate so quickly. And by then there was Sharla. . . ." His voice lowered with emotion. "Sharla. And I was in love, truly in love, for the first time in my life."

She studied his averted face and she understood. Because of Gannon she understood at last.

"It's a kind of madness, isn't it?" she asked wisely, wryly. "It takes over your life and your mind, and you have no control whatsoever over what you do."

His eyes jerked up and he studied her for a long time. "You wouldn't have said that three months ago."

She shook her head. "I didn't know three months ago what it was to love. I was so superior to the rest of the world, you know."

He laughed softly. "Were you?"

"Smug and superior. . . . I could do without anyone. I'd lost Mandy, and the world along with her. I hated you." She searched his tired face. "Helen said that Sharla doesn't have any children of her own."

There was a tiny rustling movement from the doorway, and the older woman stopped just short of Dana.

"She does . . . now," Sharla said hesitantly, her hands lifting unsurely, her face quiet, hopeful.

With a tiny, aching cry, Dana ran into those thin

arms and felt them enclose her, hold her, cradle her. And she cried until she thought her heart would break, because this woman was the mother she'd always wanted—needed. Without being disloyal to Mandy, whom she'd loved and whom she missed, Sharla was suddenly the rainbow after the storm.

Jack Steele cleared his throat, moving forward to separate the two women. "Let's eat something first," he murmured. "I can't cry on an empty stomach."

"Oh, Dad." Dana laughed through her tears and hugged him.

"Welcome home," he whispered huskily. "Welcome home, little girl."

It was the most wonderful night Dana could remember in years, sitting with her father and stepmother, learning about them, being with them. They were so good together, so secure in their love for each other. Her opinion of marriage underwent a startling change just from watching them.

Jack didn't ask any pointed questions about the time Dana had been on the coast, but just before they left Helen's house, the two of them walked out ahead of the others and she felt him watching her.

"Helen said you were nursing a blind man," he said after a minute.

"Yes. Gannon van der Vere."

He whistled. "Quite a corporate giant, Mr. van der Vere. He's regained his sight, hasn't he? I saw him on the news the other night."

She nodded. "Yes, he's . . . he's back at work."

"And quite a changed man," he added dryly.

"Don't look at me—I was just his nurse."

"Really?" He turned, holding her gaze. "You love him, don't you?"

"Desperately," she admitted, feeling a surge of hunger so sweeping that it very nearly made her swoon.

"And how does he feel?"

She lifted her shoulders. "There's a woman. . . . They were very nearly engaged before his accident. Now they're back together again. He . . . he loves her, you see."

"I'm sorry," he told her. "Very sorry."

"Don't be. Loving him was an experience I'll never forget. It's enriched my life. In so many ways."

"Yes, I can see that," he replied surprisingly. "You're very different now, Dana. Another woman from the one who left Ashton those weeks ago."

She smiled. "A better one, I hope."

He grinned. "Why don't you go back down there and put a ring on his finger?"

She laughed. "Sounds simple, doesn't it? I'm afraid he's not that kind of man. Our worlds are very different."

"Worlds," he informed her, "can merge."

"Like yours and Sharla's?" she teased. Impulsively she hugged him. "I like my new stepmother."

"She likes you too. Let's not drift apart again," he added solemnly. "Let's be a family."

She nodded. "I'd like that very much."

"Dinner with us next Friday?" he asked.

She smiled. "Ask Sharla first."

"Sharla, can we have Dana to dinner next Friday?" he called.

"Don't be silly!" was the instant reply. "My daughter can come to dinner anytime she pleases without having to have invitations. Right, Dana?"

"Right . . . Mom," she replied softly.

Sharla smiled and turned quickly away, but not before Dana caught the gleam of tears in her eyes.

In the weeks that followed, Dana became a real part of the Steele family, and her life became bright and meaningful as she threw herself back into her work. But the longer she was away from Gannon, the worse the loneliness became.

When Lorraine called her unexpectedly one Wednesday evening, she felt shock wash over her. She'd only been thinking about Gannon and his stepmother a few minutes earlier.

"How are you, my dear?" Lorraine asked softly. "We haven't heard from you, and I just wanted to check and make sure you were all right. How is your aunt?"

Her aunt. The white lie. Dana swallowed. "Oh, Aunt Helen is much better," she said. "And I'm fine too. How about you?"

"I'm doing very well. You know that Gannon could see; you saw him on television? I meant to write you, but I was so excited, and then Dirk came back to help on the computer project. . . . The house has been overrun with technicians and scientists!"

"I heard about the new invention. I'm so pleased about what Gannon's done," she murmured.

"I'm shocked," Lorraine said flatly. "He's changed so. He's like another man, so caring and concerned. Except for missing you, of course."

"What?"

"Missing you."

"What about Layn?" Dana burst out.

"My dear, she brought him home from Savannah just after you left, and looked like a thundercloud. She took off in a blaze of glory and hasn't been seen since. Gannon hasn't even mentioned her."

"I don't understand," Dana said weakly. She sat down, her legs collapsing.

"Neither do I. And he wasn't staying with Layn in Savannah, by the way. Katy and Maude told on him. He was in the hospital."

"Hospital!"

"He fell, did you know?" Lorraine asked suspiciously.

"Yes," she admitted, feeling relief. "He asked me to leave and not say anything to you about his sight returning. It puzzled me at the time. . . ."

"It's still puzzling me. I tried to pump his doctor, but I can't get anyone to tell me anything. Something's going on, Dana," she added quietly. "Something very strange. He doesn't look at women—not at all. And when he isn't working, he walks along the beach for hours at a time, looking so lonely that I ache for him."

"Maybe he misses Layn," Dana suggested.

"When he talks about no one except you?" Lorraine asked sadly. "My dear, he got his hands on a picture of you and he sits and stares at it like a starving man."

Her heart went wild. "A picture of me? Where?"

"He charmed Mrs. Pibbs out of it," Lorraine laughed. "I don't know where she found it."

Dana did. Mrs. Pibbs had asked for a photograph of her to add to some kind of brochure. Dana had thought it was an unusual request at the time, but she hadn't questioned it. And it had been for Gannon!

"Is he having any trouble at all with his eyes?" Dana asked quickly.

"No, that's the strange thing. No headaches, no blurring, no nothing. But he won't talk about that."

Dana sighed. "No, I don't suppose he likes remembering it."

"Why don't you come down for the weekend?" Lorraine asked.

Dana felt her pulse go sky high. "I don't think—"

"That's right, dear, don't think. Just come. You might consider going to see Dr. Shane while you're about it—and mention that you're going to be nursing Gannon and ask about procedure."

Dana gasped. "That would be highly unethical . . ." she began.

"Of course it would," Lorraine agreed. "But it

would get the truth out of him. I'll take full responsibility. I've got to know, Dana, I've got to!"

She paused, hanging on to the receiver as if it were a lifejacket. "Well . . ." she began, her heart racing.

"Be daring," Lorraine taunted. "Don't you want to know what he's hiding? Dana, he loves you!"

Her eyes closed at the sound of those words. *He loves you.* Heaven knew, she loved him—desperately! *God forgive me,* she murmured silently.

"I'll be there in the morning, after I get through at Dr. Shane's. Could you . . . sort of call him and pave the way?"

Lorraine laughed softly. "My dear, I'd be delighted. I won't tell Gannon, but I'll make sure he doesn't leave the house. Have a safe trip, darling."

"See you soon," she replied, and hung up. She was doing the right thing. But if Gannon was hiding something, she had to know what it was. She couldn't let him throw away their happiness without a sound reason. And nothing would be sound enough if it kept her from him—not now, when she knew how horrible life was going to be without him.

Chapter Twelve

Dana had anticipated some problems getting days off to go to the coast, but Mrs. Pibbs waved her off with a rare smile.

"The hospital will run as usual without you, Nurse," she said smoothly.

"How can I thank you . . . ?" Dana began.

"Be happy," came the reply, sincerely. "Let me know how things work out."

Dana frowned slightly. "Have you been talking to Mrs. van der Vere by any chance?" she asked suspiciously.

"Now, why in the world should you think that?" Mrs. Pibbs asked tartly. "Run along and catch your bus, Dana, I'm a busy woman. Have a nice time."

"Thank you," Dana murmured, pausing at the door. "Are you sure . . . ?"

"I'm sure. Good-bye, have a good trip."

She was suspicious about that pleasant grin, but she waved and closed the door behind her.

The hospital was crowded when she reached the coast, and she had to wait an hour before she was allowed in to see Dr. Shane.

He looked harassed and not a little irritable, but he waved her into a chair and sat down heavily.

"Thank God," he muttered, "a chance to breathe. I understand from Lorraine that you're back to nurse Gannon? God knows why, nothing's going to change regardless of your nursing skill, but who am I to argue with him? I never get anywhere at all."

Dana almost grinned but caught herself in time. She folded her hands in the lap of her green shift with its pale green belt, feeling the nails bite into her palms.

"Exactly what is his situation, Dr. Shane?" she asked with forced calm.

He pursed his lips, studying her under a frown. "Lorraine assured me that you were here with Gannon's permission," he observed. "You do realize that if that weren't the case, I'd be breaching his confidence and my oath as well?"

She swallowed. "Yes, sir," she said. It was on the tip of her tongue to tell the truth, to be honest, but something kept her quiet and still.

He shrugged. "Very well, I'll have to take Lorraine's word for it. I wasn't even aware that he'd told her. But then, he's a strange man at times."

He pulled a file toward him and opened it. "You know that the shrapnel is inoperable?"

"Yes, sir," she said, which was the truth. She sat stiffly, waiting.

"Well, nothing's changed there. The fall was a stroke of good luck, because it dislodged the shrapnel and relieved the pressure, returning his vision. However," he said, leaning back in the chair solemnly, to pin her with his eyes, "he has no guarantee that the same thing won't happen again and leave him blind."

Her heart stopped—stopped and then ran away. "He could become blind again?" she echoed numbly.

"Of course. There are new advances, you know. Every day we learn more and can do more. But for the present he has to go on living with that sword hanging over him."

"If the shrapnel shifts again," she said slowly, "it could do more than blind him, couldn't it?"

He lifted his hands. "As a nurse, you know as well as I do that anything lodged in the brain is a potential time bomb. But there's nothing medical science can do about it at the present time. I wish that weren't the case. But I'm afraid it is."

"And naturally," she continued, in what seemed a terribly slow voice, "he wouldn't want to ask anyone to share that risk with him."

"Marriage, you mean," he nodded. He sighed. "He said almost that same thing himself. I told him he was being absurd, but he wouldn't listen. Good heavens, Nurse, I could step off a curb and kill myself tomorrow, and there's nothing lodged in my brain!"

She managed a wan smile. "How very odd that he wanted to keep it to himself."

"Not odd at all. It's like him." He closed the file. "Well, that's all I can tell you, unless you want me to read you the medical terminology. He shouldn't participate in any daredevil antics, of course, and things like diving and violent sports are out. Otherwise he can lead a fairly normal life."

"A sneeze could dislodge it, couldn't it?" she asked quietly.

"Yes. Few people outside the medical profession realize how violent a sneeze is." He watched her pale face with interest. "The best thing is not to dwell on it and not to let *him* dwell on it. There's a man in Vienna working on innovations in brain surgery right now; I expect a breakthrough any day. When it comes—and notice I said when, not if—I'll get in touch with Gannon."

She smiled weakly. "Thank you for telling me."

"Does Gannon know you're here?" he asked kindly.

"If I were here under false pretenses, would I answer that?" she asked, standing.

"No. So I'd better not ask." He took her hand. "Blast him out of his prison, girl. No man has the right to sacrifice himself on a gamble. That piece of shrapnel could stay where it is until he's a hundred and ten years old, for all you or I know."

She nodded. "Now all I have to do is convince

him of that." Her eyes darkened. "If I don't murder him first," she added coldly.

He chuckled softly. "Let me know how things work out. I love happy endings."

"His may not be so happy," she muttered, gathering speed as she walked out the door, thanking him again before she went stalking down the hall.

She took a cab to the beach house, fuming. He was going to spend the rest of his life living alone because of something that might happen. He was going to make her, and himself, miserable and shut her out of his life and deny her even the choice of staying or going. The more she thought about it, the madder she got. By the time she paid the cab and walked to the front door of the beach house, her face was hot with temper.

Lorraine answered it, and her thin face lit up. She grabbed Dana like a long-lost daughter. "Oh, I was so afraid you'd change your mind, back out. I'm just beside myself that you came anyway!"

"I'm glad too," she replied, hugging Lorraine back. "Dr. Shane told me everything. It's the shrapnel. He could become blind again."

The older woman closed her eyes with a sigh. "So that's it. It explains so much."

"Yes, it does. But it doesn't justify sending me away if he really does care," she added, frowning, because she wasn't sure that he did. She couldn't be.

"If you'll take an old woman's word," Lorraine said softly, "I think he does. Very much."

Dana sighed, afraid now, because the anger was wearing off and leaving desperation in its place. She could have misread the entire situation. It might be Layn he was sparing, not Dana.

"Why don't you walk down to the beach and find him?" Lorraine suggested, her eyes kind. "I think you'll be able to tell one way or another the minute he sees you. What he feels will be in his face, because he isn't expecting you and he won't be prepared."

Dana's heart leaped. "He's on the beach?"

Lorraine nodded. "About halfway down, sitting on a log, glowering at the ocean. Go on. Be daring. What have you got to lose?"

There was the question. She had nothing to lose, because without Gannon there was nothing she minded losing. She pulled her shoulders back and laid her purse down on the hall table.

"Wish me luck, will you?" she asked the older woman. "I think I may need it."

"All the luck in the world, my dear." Lorraine gave her a push. "Go on. You'll never know until you face him."

"I may see you again very soon."

"If you don't, I won't wait lunch," came the dry reply.

Dana walked through the house and down the back steps with her heart hammering wildly at her throat. She paused at the top of the staircase that led down to the beach, and looked down until her eyes found Gannon.

His back was to her. He was wearing white slacks

and a blue and white patterned tropical shirt, and his head was bowed in the sunlight. He looked so alone, so bitterly alone, that she felt like crying. That gave her the courage she needed to go down the steps and walk along the beach toward him. Her heart was hammering wildly at her throat like a trapped bird trying to be free, while the waves crashed onto the beach and the sun burned down on the white sand.

Dana's footsteps were muffled by the sound of the surf as she approached the big blond man sitting on the log. Her breath seemed to catch in her throat. Would he be glad to see her? Or would he just be shocked and annoyed?

She paused just behind him. Her hand lifted and then fell. "Gannon?" she called softly.

His head jerked up. When he saw her, he seemed to go rigid all over. His eyes took her in from head to toe and back again, noting the emerald-green dress, her face in its frame of pale, loosened hair, her wide, searching eyes.

"Dana?" he whispered, standing.

"Yes," she said simply. Her own eyes were busy reconciling the man she saw with her memory of him. He looked thinner somehow, worn, but the sight of him fed her poor, starved eyes.

"What are you doing here?" he asked.

"I, uh, I came to see Lorraine," she hedged, words failing her.

His chest rose and fell heavily. "Was that the only reason?"

Her lower lip trembled and she caught it between her teeth. "No," she replied with a shaky smile. "I . . . came to see you too."

"You look very thin," he said in a tight voice, studying her slenderness again. "Is that new?"

"The dress? No, it's an old one."

"The thinness, not the dress," he said harshly. "Why should I care about what you wear?"

"Why should you care about me, period?" she burst out, anger coming to her rescue. "Not a single phone call, not a card. . . . I could have died and you wouldn't have known or cared!"

"That's a lie," he shot back, his face pale. "I kept up with you through Mrs. Pibbs. I knew how you were, at least. You couldn't even be bothered to write to Lorraine, could you?"

"Why should I, when you sent me away?" she tossed back, hurting all the way to her bones. "You sent me away!"

"I had to," he ground out, his face contorting as he saw the hurt in her eyes. "You don't understand."

"Yes, I do," she cried angrily. "You sent me away because of the shrapnel!"

He looked every year of his age. His powerful frame seemed to shudder. "Who told you?" he asked in a deadly quiet tone.

"I won't tell you," she returned. "But it's true, isn't it? You could go blind again."

His eyes closed on a weary sigh. "Yes," he said heavily. "I could go blind again."

She moved closer, looking up at him with soft, probing eyes. "I have to know," she said quietly. "I haven't much pride left—or much sense. I have to be told. Was it because of Layn that you wanted me to break the engagement, Gannon? Was it because of my scar . . . ?"

He whispered something rough under his breath and his hands shot out. With an expression of pure anguish he dragged her against his big body and bent to her mouth.

"Don't talk," he said unsteadily, brushing his lips slowly, tremblingly, over hers. "Don't talk. Kiss me. Let me show you how it's been without you, Dana!"

She bent under the rough crush of his ardor, feeling the hurt and the heartache and the loneliness all wrapped up in his slow, fierce kisses. She clung to him with tears draining from her eyes, loving the touch of him, the feel and smell and taste of him, as the world seemed to turn to gold all around them, binding them together with skeins of pure love.

"I missed you," he whispered brokenly, wrapping her up in his big arms to rock her slowly against him. "I've been half a man since the day I sent you away. But I couldn't let you stay, knowing what I did. I only wanted what was best for you."

She hit his broad chest with a small, furious fist. "You stupid man," she whimpered, burying her face against him. "As if I cared about being protected. I'm a nurse, not an hysterical woman. And I love you quite desperately, in case you haven't noticed. You wouldn't even let me have a choice!"

"How could I, knowing what the choice would be?" he ground out, holding her even closer. "Dana, you're so young, with your whole life ahead of you."

"What kind of life am I expected to have, for heaven's sake, without you?" she asked in anguish, lifting her red eyes to his. "Don't you even know that I only go through the motions of living without you? There'll never be anyone else, not as long as I live. So please tell me how to look forward to a lifetime of loneliness and grief—because I'll mourn you every day I live from now on!"

He tried to speak and made a helpless motion with his shoulders before he dragged her close again and bent his head over hers.

"I could die," he whispered.

"Yes," she managed on a sob. "So could I. A tree could fall on me while I was walking back to the house. Do you think life comes with a written guarantee?"

"I could be paralyzed."

"Then I'd sit with you," she whispered, lifting her head to study him with love pouring from her face. "I'd sit by your bedside and hold your hand and read to you. And I'd love you so much. . . ."

The tears burst from his eyes and ran unashamedly down his cheeks as she spoke, and she reached up and tenderly touched each of them, brushing them back from his hard cheeks.

"I love you," she repeated softly, blinking away her own tears. "If we got married, I could give you children. And then, even if something dreadful did happen, we'd have all those happy years behind us; we'd have the comfort of our family around us. We'd have each other and the memory of loving."

He bent and kissed her eyes softly, slowly. "I love you," he whispered, shaken. "So much that I'd willingly give up my life for you. But what am I offering you except the possibility of a living nightmare?"

"If you won't marry me," she said after a minute, "I'll live with you anyway. I'll move in and sleep in your arms and shame you for not making an honest woman of me." She drew back and looked up into his darkening eyes. "I'll follow you around like a puppy from now on, and you won't be able to look behind you without seeing me. I'll crawl on my knees if I have to, but I won't leave you now. Not until I die."

"Dana, for God's sake . . ."

"It *is* for God's sake," she whispered softly, smiling. "For God's sake and my own. Because all I know of love I learned from you."

His eyes closed. "Don't make it any harder for me," he pleaded.

"But I will," she replied, snuggling closer, feeling safe and secure for the first time in weeks. "You've given me back my family. Because I loved you, I was able to forgive them and love them again. I'm part of a family again, all because of you."

"I don't want you hurt," he whispered.

"Then don't send me away," she whispered back. She drew his face down to hers. "Because I'll never be hurt again if I can stay where you are."

"It's insane," he ground out against her warm, soft mouth.

She smiled. "Yes," she murmured. "Sweet insanity. Kiss me. Then I'll propose to you again and go and ask your mother for your hand in marriage. . . ."

He burst out laughing in spite of himself. "Dana, you crazy woman . . . !"

"Be crazy with me," she tempted. She stood on tiptoe and kissed him again. And then she felt his arms contract, and he was kissing her. It was a long time before they could find words again.

"This isn't solving anything," he said finally, dragging himself away from her. "Here, sit down and let's try to talk reasonably."

She joined him on the log, sitting close, companionably, while he took a deep breath and sat, just looking at her.

"You look so different," he murmured.

"From my photograph, you mean?" she replied with an impish smile.

He shifted and looked uncomfortable for a minute. "Who told you? Lorraine?"

"Don't blame her," she pleaded. "I was clutching at straws. I thought you'd forgotten all about me."

He shook his head. "That was beyond me. I've sat here day after day, remembering the sound and smell of you." His eyes searched her quiet face and he smiled. "You're the most beautiful thing I've seen since I regained my sight."

She blushed and lowered her eyes. "I'm very glad that you think so." She glanced up again, warily. "Gannon, the scar . . ."

He bent and brushed the soft hair away from her cheek and kissed the pale white line that ran alongside her ear. "We'll think of it as a beauty mark," he whispered. "We'll tell the children that you got it fighting tigers in Malaya, just to make it sound better."

Her eyes searched his. "You're going to let me stay?" she asked softly.

He touched her mouth with his fingers. "How can I let you go now?" he asked quietly. "But we may both live to regret it, Dana."

She shook her head. "Not ever."

She said it with such conviction that he averted his eyes on a heavy, ragged sigh. He caught her hand in his and held it tightly.

"I saw you on television," she mentioned, grinning. "You looked so handsome—my roommate said you were a dish."

He chuckled. "I didn't feel like a dish. I was missing you and hurting in ways I hadn't dreamed I could."

"Me and not Layn?"

He looked haunted for an instant, and the big hand holding hers contracted roughly. "I needed something to drive you away when Dr. Shane told me the truth. I couldn't bear the thought of subjecting you to what might happen." He shrugged.

"It seemed the thing to do at the time. I knew you'd never go if you knew the truth." He glanced down at her. "You're far too caring a person to desert a sinking ship."

She nuzzled close to him, sighing. "You never really cared about her, then?"

"No. And she knew it—she knew exactly what I was doing. I'm still not sure why she went along with it, unless she thought she might have a chance with me again." He lifted his hand and let it fall. "She found out pretty quickly that she didn't. By that time I was so much in love with you that I couldn't see her for dust."

"There was something strange in your voice when you called me from Savannah," she confessed. "I couldn't help wondering at the time if you were really telling me the truth about being able to see again."

"Oh, I could see all right. And not just in any visual sense," he added on a hard sigh. "I could see you living with this time bomb in my head."

"We all carry time bombs around with us, Gannon," she said gently. "Of one kind or another. None of us knows the hour of our own death. It's just as well too: We'd never accomplish anything. You might survive me."

"Horrible thought," he said curtly. He looked down at her with all his heart in his eyes. "I wouldn't want to live without you."

"But you were going to condemn me to it, weren't you?" she accused. She reached up and touched his face as she'd longed to for so many empty weeks. "I want you to come home with me and meet my father and my stepmother and my aunt. I think—I hope—you'll like them."

"You've made your peace, I see," he observed.

She smiled. "I found that I quite like my stepmother. She's just what my father needed. I kind of like him too. We cleared up a lot of misunderstandings; we're closer now than ever before. And best of all, I've come to grips with my own guilt and my grief. I'll always miss my mother, but I realize now that she's better off."

"God does know best," he murmured, smiling at the look on her face. "Oh, yes, I've done my bit of changing. I've realized that there's much more to life than the making and spending of money."

She reached up and kissed him. "I've arrived at the same conclusion. When are you going to marry me?"

"You've only just proposed," he reminded her. "A man can't be rushed into these things, after all. I have to buy a suit and have my hair done. . . ."

"Stop that," she muttered, hitting him lovingly.

"Well, if you don't mind an untidy bridegroom, I suppose we could get married Monday."

"That's only three days away!" she gasped.

He shrugged. "Well, we can do it sooner, I suppose; I just thought . . ."

"Monday is fine!" she said quickly, laughing. "Oh, Monday is just fine!"

"Then let's go call my minister and see about

getting a license," he said. He stood up, drawing her with him. "Lovely, lovely woman. I'm the luckiest man alive."

"You're certainly the handsomest," she murmured. "What gorgeous sons we'll have!"

He chuckled, leading her down the beach. "Our daughters aren't going to be bad, either," he observed.

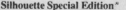